Simple Conversation

A NOVEL

Sonia Rumzi

Heart Press
Sausalito, CA

First Edition Feb 2011

For information about special discounts for bulk purchases, please contact Heart Press Special Sales at business@heartpress.com

Design by Stefano

Manufactured in the United States of America

Library of Congress Cataloging-in-Publication Data on request
 Library of Congress Control Number: 2010918825

Rumzi, Sonia, 1956-
       Simple Conversation: a novel / by Sonia Rumzi

ISBN-13: 978-0-9831978-0-5
ISBN-10:   0-9831978-0-6

To my husband,
Steve,
of course,
without you,
I could not.

Acknowledgements

This book was a project of love, written with joy and excitement. There are several people, I would like to thank, for making this project, a success:

My main editor and close friend, Arthur Hoffman, whose red pen, covered all the pages; thoroughly, and so completely. Thank you for taking the time, to make me a better writer. Thank you, for being, my friend.

My daughter, Nadya, 1st Sergeant, in the U.S Marine Corps, for reading, editing and commenting on the raw files. For taking the time. You are my treasure.

My daughter, Sherry Forde, dedicated Mother extraordinaire, for her amazing illustrations. You are talented and beautiful. Thank you for taking the time to do those drawings for me.

My friend, Denise, for reading and commenting on, my, yet to be published, novel. Thank you for your friendship and the follow through.

My friends, Gary and Pat, for your kindness and generosity. Allowing me time, in your home, at Sea Ranch, you gave me the space, the inspiration and the quiet, needed, for this project to be completed. Thank you.

To my friend Jason, Master Sergeant in the US Marine Corps, for his creative suggestion for the cover. Without you, it would have been, just another cover. Thank you.

To my publisher, Heart Press, you light up my life.

Simple
Conversation

PRELUDE
HOW IT STARTED

THE AD

Subject: Conversation! - 47   Thu Sep 11 2003
Reply to: anon-emailer@craigslist.org

"I miss good conversation. If you can write well and wish to have an e-pal, I would be very interested".

Salma did not intend to fall in love.

Having moved to Sausalito for work, she had no intention of staying. No intentions of dating either, long, or short term. She just missed talking to men.

Since she found her apartment on Craigslist, that, is where she wrote, her personal ad.

The ad was received with hate and enthusiasm. She received 37 e-mail responses. 31, basically told her, to get a life and come out from behind her computer. One even suggested that she is fat and ugly, hmmmmm. Also that "conversation is face to face, what are you afraid of?"

Why they bothered, really, was beyond her understanding. Why not just ignore the ad, pass over it, leave it alone. No, everyone had something to say.

Three of the answers included pictures, which she disregarded immediately. It seemed that that portion of the population did not get it. She was not interested in what they looked like, she would have included her own picture, if she was interested . She really wanted to know what they had to say.

Only the last three seemed reasonable. She smiled thinking how snobbish and obnoxious she sounded, even to herself. She answered all three e-mails.

Several e-mails later she was talking to just one person... Merrick.

WRITING

The minute I heard my first love story I started
looking for you, not knowing how blind that was.
Lovers don't finally meet somewhere. They're in each
other all along.

- Rumi

In the interest of keeping things as close to the truth as possible, none of the e-mails were changed or doctored. Most people do not re-read their e-mails, hence, the mistakes, the errors and the horrific punctuation.

Our heroine was no different. Neither was her correspondent who answered believing that he also, could speak the language.

Advance apologies to the ones, sensitive to grammatical errors and atrocious language. Salma's experience with Merrick was the intention of the story.

Subject: Interests?   *Thu Sep 11 2003*
To: anon-emailer@craigslist.org   *From: Searcher*

Dearest Scribe,
What interests are important?

Subject: Re: Interests?   *Thu Sep 11 2003*
To: Searcher   *From: The Scribe*

Movies... games... books... life... experiences... feelings... the weather... surroundings... exercise... nutrition....

No really, I am not that boring! But I can be. What is the latest movie you have seen? I last saw Dirty Pretty Things, very disturbing!

The Scribe

Subject: Re: Interests?   *Fri Sep 12 2003*
To: The Scribe   *From: Searcher*

>What is the latest movie you have seen?<

LOL. Ohhh it figures, of all the questions you might ask, you pick this. I see maybe 3-4 films a year, at best. This year, the one I enjoyed the most was Pixar's Finding Nemo. As a computer support geek, I find a great deal of inspiration in what artists can do within the digital art form. Bowling for Columbine was by design adversarial, lacking something of heart - but I liked it too.

I'm a fiery 43, with a personality program running that allows me to hide behind my perceived uniqueness, or so I've been told. What I do know about my existence is how I'm not usually seen as a prototypical male.

>Movies... games... books... life... experiences... feelings... the weather... surroundings... exercise... nutrition....

From your laundry list:
movies, covered.
games, don't play.

books, read all sorts of stuff.

experiences, don't get me started.

feelings, see male comment above.

weather, global shift.

surroundings, north of SF.

exercise, body & mind.

nutrition, healthy.

Okay, with that out of the way, what's your take on the approaching spirituality of machines?

What do you find more exciting to play with, analog or digital?

One for instance; do you believe Ray Kurzweil's digital understandings, or does the biological realm keep your attention? If you don't know what I'm speaking of, try these links for some "light" reading:

http://www.kurzweilai.net/the-law-of-accelerating-returns

http://www.kurzweilai.net/prologue-an-inexorable-emergence

I commute long distances on a bus each workday, so there's often a chance to write - thus your offer sounded intriguing. The places I find most fascinating are the humanist themes within accelerating change. Can we assist, especially when the very fabric is yanked away, leaving a naked & fearful society in its wake?

How was your week?

Merrick

Subject: Re: Interests?   *Sat Sep 13 2003*
From: The Scribe   *To: Searcher*

Thank you for those articles.... :-) If you were trying to impress me with your intelligence and my lack of understanding therefore putting me in place for suggesting that I want intelligent conversation, you may have succeeded.

But truthfully, I will read those and let you know what I think or was that not the point?

You base all your life on science don't you! If you cannot see it or cannot understand it mentally then it either does not exist or there must be a flaw in it. Interesting! I like the fact that you believe that you are somehow unique or special in some way, I am sure that makes you feel good or better anyway about hiding behind your computer.

There is nothing more exciting and revealing than to allow one to be naked and open in their soul and spirit so that we could see within ourselves. I refuse to believe that the human spirit is that fragile that when all is revealed we will be left with fear and uncertainty.

Humans are probably the only creatures who know that they will die. They know for certain and yet they keep going. A resilient spirit and a need to survive does not make for cowardice.

How was your week, mine was absolutely incredible!

Regards,

Salma

Subject: *Ahhh, thank you!*   Sun Sep 14 2003
To: *The Scribe*   From: Searcher

Hi Salma,

Thank you; this is *much* better than the movies!

>my lack of understanding therefore<

Ohhh, with this note, you reveal the many depths of your understanding. My initial belief in responding to you has been justified. If I'd thought for a moment idle chit chat would be exactly what you'd asked for, well, that's not what

I'm about...

>But truthfully, I will read those and let you know what I think or was that not the point?<

And from about an hour ago, another important & similar question: why don't identical twins have matching fingerprints?

>you base all your life on science don't you!<

Actually, no. It *is* a strong frame of reference, but it's not how I base my life. I'm rather a spiritual dolt, with a drive towards knowing the unknowable, within the spiritual context, not the scientific.

>hiding behind your computer<.

I do have this ability, this is true. This doesn't mean I'm a product of a computer display. The sea's horizon has more to do with self than many realize.

>...when all is revealed we will be left with fear and uncertainty... Humans are probably the only creatures who know that they will die<

Ahhh, the crux of the matter - so quickly too.

I'm now amazed, shocked actually.

Salma, you're an interesting woman.

FWIW, who says humans die? I don't believe the "psychic energy" vanishes with each passing; there's a theory of matter that says nothing within the material realm disappears. It may change in form & substance, but the intrinsic value of the material remains in one form or another. It's my belief the same holds true for who we are as well.

>How was your week, mine was absolutely incredible!<

I'm currently filling the well at a highly technical conference this weekend, where the most interesting track for me is Humanism. The others in Science, Technology, and Business have some weight, but it's the social implications of

Accelerating Change I find so captivating…
   A good week here! Why was yours so incredible?
   Blessings,
   Merrick

Subject: Ahhh, thank you!   *Sun Sep 14 2003*
To: Searcher   *From: The Scribe*

Good Morning Merrick!

Thank you for the kind words and encouragement. I think I agree that we do not "die" in the sense that we disappear, far from it. But then, we get into religion and faith and belief systems.

Are you ready for that?? I have found that most people will want to talk spirituality if it is presented to them in the context that they are comfortable with. If I truly say my beliefs, then I am narrow or not flexible or some other label.

I am glad because it seems that you understood my hesitation in starting our conversations with "Do you believe…."

Movies seemed the simplest way to start…:-) I let people take me where they want to, I am an easy follower and that way I learn so much more.

My week was wonderful because I live moment to moment. I have a rather simple life. I have no belongings. I have no credit cards, if I don't have the money I do not buy it. I have no debt. My car is a rental from work. My clothes are few. My sentences are short ….hehehehehe! Better than Dickens who went on and on and on and…..
   Salma

Subject: Re: Ahhh, thank you!　　　　　　*Sun Sep 14 2003*
To: The Scribe　　　　　　　　　　　　　*From: Searcher*

>we get into religion and faith and belief systems<.

Agreed. As discoveries continue to unfold, science as well, which is the why in this weekend's conference.

>Are you ready for that??<

Of course I am, even though I mentioned in my first note how you shouldn't get me started. ;-)

>If I truly say my beliefs, then... some other label.<

You know you're not the label; that's the product of another's perception, especially when trying to communicate using this limiting language. Real communication doesn't make these distinctions, and by this, isn't language based.

>I am an easy follower and that way I learn so much more.<

Listening & trying to gain another's understanding does this for me, but I'm not by nature a follower. Let me rephrase that, I haven't found many folks I'd be willing to follow. If someone were to appear, well, she'd likely be unique...

>I have no belongings... if I don't have the money I do not buy it.<

So with the above, will you admit to being a walking, breathing paradox? If you buy things, then by the very nature of our consumer based society, you have belongings. I fully understand the spirit in what you've said, more in a moment.

>I have no debt... My clothes are few.<

Now you're toying with me; a woman with few clothes? No debt?

Hummmm, okay, if you have clothes, then you're not a

9

female sadhu, at least not in a fully traditional sense. Ah, a label appears! green skinned, sent to unravel the male psyche, "alien"...

Congrats on your achievements; I'm getting there, but it's been a slow struggle. Past karmic deposits have been so challenging. I built a white picket fence life, because it was the expected path of "happily married" compromise.

I've got to run along, the clock keeps ticking, and I'm a bit hungry too.

An open soul is such a rare gift.

Yes, it's been a particularly good week.

With love,

Merrick

Subject: An open soul!   Sun Sep 14 2003
To: Searcher   *From: The Scribe*

I admit I got caught on that one. You are absolutely right. I do buy things therefore I do have things. :-) I did not say that I do not have anything, I said that I do not own anything. I do not need to protect anything from loss, nothing is worth the trouble to me... if they want it, they can have it.

My clothes are necessities and I admit some frivolous things also because I am still female. I love shawls and soft clothes. I just bought my first pair of jeans a few months ago. Mostly, I wear dresses and skirts. At work, I wear scrubs, so life is easy in that way.

Your weekend conference sounds very interesting. I wish I was there to listen but maybe you can share some of the content with me.

Merrick?? How old are you? You seem so young to me.

Love back,

Salma

Subject: Re: An open soul!   *Sun Sep 14 2003*
To: The Scribe   *From: Searcher*

>I did not say that I do not have anything, I said that I do not own anything.<

LOL, semantically speaking, you claimed no belongings. Often there are many different meanings within language, which is one reason for my ambiguous feelings toward technology. It's rough enough to communicate accurately face to face, reduction to text misses soooo much - yet, has a quality that's interesting.

I still have too much, which I'm hoping eBay will be of assistance. As a kid, my father instilled an understanding how automobiles are tools, like a hammer. The Honda CRX I own is old & tired, and is due for replacement. I can no longer rely on it for long distances. Anyway, human beings don't own anything, we're stewards at best.

>maybe you can share some of the content with me.<

It's going to take some time to digest & contemplate the weekend's numerous presentations. There's plenty to share, and at some point, DVDs should become available. Oh, but then you don't have any belongings, so that might not be valuable.

Salma, a silly question. Do you have a computer?

With the conference completion, I can say it was absolutely a good thing for me. It didn't provide many answers or even solid directions for my personal questions, maybe in time. There's so much to consider.

>Merrick?? How old are you? you seem so young to me.<

Well thank you; I think. Aries males aren't usually old & slow! 43 chronologically, 4/15/60.

This is an interesting observation. My age isn't usually guessed at as being young. I can assure you, biological regression isn't something I've mastered. However, if I could keep some knowledge & have my 20 year old body again, Danger Will Robinson, Danger.

>I am still female.<

Female body yes, but here's another big question for introspection; how much do you know of your maleness?

That's plenty for now.

Merrick

Hello Merrick!

I have been smiling like an idiot for the last few minutes reading your message. you are very witty and your writing is funny and poignant. I find myself reading it several times to grasp some of what you say and when I get it, I smile!

By the way, I happen to be an Aries also 04/16/56. What do they say about Aries women? So, you have met an Aries woman, huh? I am not sure whether to congratulate you or feel sorry for you. I am also a fire monkey in the Chinese calendar, hence I am egotistical, egocentric, showy, opinionated, theatrical and self-centered.

With age I have managed to temper some of those traits-!!

Am I aware of my maleness?? You would be surprised! I have been told by several men that if they wanted to date a man, they would have become gay...being with me that is! It comes from being on the reasonable side, I do not throw temper tantrums, I reason, I listen, I allow for errors. Yes, I am very aware of it.

Yes, I do have a computer that was given to me as a gift by a lover. It is a SONY VAIO and it is not in proper working condition right now. I am using it strictly for DVD watching...lol!

I live on the premise that what I have does not belong to me. When there is a need I try and meet it. My paycheck belongs to the most need. I am not sure how to explain that without sounding "giving" which is not what I am portraying. I do it out of a selfish desire to remain blessed and living on the shirttails of that blessing and living well.

I am sorry that the conference did not meet your needs or that it did not live up to what it was supposed to accomplish.

Did I happen to mention that I am originally Egyptian?? I was born and raised and married in Egypt and came to the States when I was 22.

Sincerely,
Salma

Subject: Re: Ode to laughter   Mon Sep 15 2003
To: The Scribe   *From: Searcher*

>I happen to be an Aries also...<

Oh Goddess of Joyous Upheaval, please help us! We do not know what we do!

>04/16/56.<

Might this be a source for your earlier impression how I'm sooooo "young"? My most precious relationships have always been with older women. :-)

>I am also a fire monkey in the Chinese calendar<

As you can see, I'm a RAT, so please read into that what you will! From what I can tell, I'm everything I've read, and work my buns off to remain an indigenous chameleon.

>Yes, I am very aware of it.<

LOL - No wonder your words were "still female", because I'm still male too - I think. Silk is my absolute favorite fabric, with today's cotton/silk blend pants as a typical & comfortable "normal".

When it was pointed out how silk worms can be exploited, moral dilemmas abound. I haven't purchased any new silk items since. I'm still contemplating how to resolve this. Silk is soooo good for me, assisting me thermally, emotionally, and likely spiritually too. If it's exploitative, <sigh>

I haven't owned a pair of jeans in 25 years. Also, if you're harboring any beliefs how I might be like other depicted "typical" male types, I'm not usually described as a manly man. I've never had any desire to be a fully ripped, testosterone powered, gym junkie.

Rob Brezsny's book, "The Tele-visionary Oracle", is a strange guidebook of sorts for me; as a macho feminist, I believe in women's rights, and diminishing the continuing male oppressiveness. At the same time, yes I fully admit it, this body/mind combination is entranced by female flowers.

>...living on the shirttails of that blessing and living well.<

I find this to be a difficult balance.

Needs arise & often paradoxically.

>I am sorry that the conference did not meet your needs or that it did not live up to what it was supposed to accomplish.<

It met my needs in exciting & strange ways, so that's not really what I'm saying. For months I've been sleeping less well, wondering "what's next" for me; what direction would be most harmonious for my Tevas to take me toward. Here's one for instance out of many; the company I work for has furthered my publishing experience & support capabilities, continues to pay off my remaining debt, *and* is slowly draining the life out of me. I knew this would happen going into this workplace, but it's been a necessary compromise.

At the same time, there's little this company creates that's vital, and the conference reinforced this fact yet again. So, at some point, an answer to this & many other lingering personal issues will gain in clarity. This is kinda what I meant by "personal" needs. It's difficult to explain in text like this.

>Did I happen to mention that I am originally Egyptian??<

I'll try to ask this "differently". Do you find yourself aligning along any traditional pathways today, I.e. yes the stuff like; faith, religion, beliefs…

Originally, my childhood was started with some Christian teachings, and then around age 10 or so, evolved into little more than experiential dis-involvement with all religious folks. More recent history means I've studied with the Pagans, Tibetans, other Buddhists, the Sun, the Moon, just about any & all. The question arises from your birthplace roots. Were you a part of the modern consumer culture, or within a more traditional foundation. I'm always curious how folks get to where they are, by way of understanding where they've been. At some point, jumping into the river & trying to stay within the current will take me to the sea's horizon.

I'm still laughing. Internal gender understanding, much less any realized balance, isn't a condition society normally creates.

May your work boots & overalls be forever blessed with rose petals.

With love,

Merrick
PS - going forward, scribe whatever feels best, because I'm usually more like an odeist novelist... until I'm not.

Subject: Re: Ode to laughter   Mon Sep 15 2003
To: Searcher   *From: The Scribe*

Merrick,
I have just finished work and it is around a little before ten and I am tired. But, I had to look at your e-mail and respond.... :-)
I will continue buying silk...sorry! My apologies to the silk worm but we are all exploited in some way or another. We all give and receive.
I may not be very coherent writing this so maybe I should wait till I am more lucid and less exhausted.... hehehehehe...I seem to be repeating the same thing but in different words. I am tired! whew!
I was raised Orthodox. Christian Egyptian with very traditional values. I broke away from those many years ago. But, I am still a believer. Are you going to run away now??
Salma

Subject: Singularity   Mon Sep 15 2003
To: The Scribe   *From: Searcher*

Good morning / afternoon / evening Salma,
I began this note during my Monday AM commute, finishing it on the ride back. It's my hope to convey something *really* important from this weekend's conference, yet it's not at all clear how to accomplish this.
My lengthy & recent yoga studies have given me a solid grounding in Patanjali's most important & first moral

discipline. The Sanskrit term is Ahimsa, which best translates to "non-harming".

I've yet to find the skillful means to speak of what's approaching, without the possibility of creating fear. Fear is exceedingly harmful, yet in my opinion, ignorance has become the greater harming influence. Yes, this is likely a justification for speaking up, but is there really a choice? We shall see.

I was heartened to find many people at the conference interested in the humanism track. In fact, our Saturday evening dessert session proved just how pervasive this was. From the dinner discussions of Business, Science, Technology, and Humanism, the most vocal during the dessert round-up were the Humanism groups. This is a good thing too, because it's the one bright light within the grayness I'm about to share.

The basic concept is easy enough to state, harder to articulate clearly, and difficult to fully understand the implications. Here are the easy words to say:

Today's growth rate towards Moral Singularity isn't equivalent or higher than that of Technical Singularity.

With the rate of technical change & innovation accelerating exponentially, life as we understand it today *will* change radically. It will also do this within our lifetimes, most likely in the next 20-30 years. Singularity, as defined by Vinge will likely happen in 50-80 years. This is the exciting, sobering, and for most who understand this, a chilling reality in which we're living today.

Laboratories today are creeping forward, figuring out how to assemble *anything* from the bottom-up, using atomic level precision. This is a great thing, maybe. For instance, imagine a tiny self-replicating machine that can split two hydrogen atoms away from an oxygen atom. This is a good thing, especially if this new & inexpensive capability removes our dependence on fossil fuels.

Now imagine this self replicating machine gets loose within nature, without proper controls & safeguards. Like most everything living, human beings are mostly water too! Within a matter of days, such a self-replicating machine could remove *all* water from the planet, saturating the atmosphere with hydrogen & oxygen. This outcome is abundantly disharmonious to what we know as "life". The results would likely be some gray goo, and a whole bunch of dry stuff. There are many other ways this gray goo cataclysm could happen using tiny tech.

Vast amounts of additional reading on the approaching singularity can be found on the net."

Salma stopped. What in the world was he talking about? So many words to say, what? That we are moving faster than we should or need to?

Grabbing her mouse, she dragged it down to see how long this e-mail would be. She was stunned at his resilience.

How much could someone say to make a point? What was the point? Our technology moving faster than our morality could keep up with was not a new concept.

Yet, she found herself drawn to his words. Why in the world was that? She was not sure that she understood everything that he said. She was not sure. Yet, she was drawn to his words like a bee to a flowering bush.

Leaning back in her chair, she looked at the words on the

screen and scrunching her face, she continued to read.

"To back up this claim of its onward advance, nothing I heard this weekend convinces me this won't happen. We can argue the overall timing of this, however, I believe, as does Ray Kurzweil & many others, there's a hidden universal law driving this upward, not mankind. Mankind is merely a willing participant to this universal process. The experts that were brought in to debate with Kurzweil didn't make a clear case to add any balance to the mix.

In fact, each trying to do so, found their arguments circling back around, further assisting Kurzweil's position. This, lack of brain powered momentum more than anything else, signals that it's most likely a universal code driving things forward. Many big brains have been contemplating this, and the only thing that seems to vary is when the approaching technical singularity will happen, not if it will. We will establish limited forms of bottom-up manufacturing soon. The big unknown is what effect this will have on the biology of the planet, including the human stewards.

Moral singularity, on the other hand, is not growing at the same pace. Many would say it's hardly changed in the last 50 years. Unlike technological innovation, the human animal has many impediments to growth, especially when it comes to lasting moral & ethical understanding. When a human is born, the moral clock starts over, where the tech clock runs continuously. It is this split, more than anything thing else, that's the greatest peril to life on this planet. For instance, today, it's a technical triviality to provide adequate food, water, sanitation, and shelter for everyone on the planet. It's not a matter of resources or money either, nothing like that. It's a lack of moral obligation & duty by those capable of doing something about it. If every first world country spent just under 1% of Gross Domestic Production to end planetary suffering of these types, including a basic education, the planet would be much more peaceful.

After some additional research, this split could be a place where I'm going to become more vocal. What I wonder is how to do this without withholding what's happening, and at the same time, not harming by creating fear. Like my workplace, this is another "personal" issue I went to this conference with, hoping to find some stepping stones. Few were uncovered, but I took one blind step of faith today. We'll see if it was unwise & I fall over a cliff in a few days.

There's so much to say about all of this stuff, yet doing so coherently, and without causing harm - might be nearly impossible. At the same time, I'm having a difficult time just letting it happen, doing nothing. If I do something, the perennial question is: what?

With love,
Merrick

Subject: Re: Is this better??   *Tue Sep 16 2003*
To: The Scribe   *From: Searcher*

>But, I am still a believer.
Dear one,
One Universal Milk, many dogmatic cows.
>Are you going to run away now??
Run, no.
Away, no.
Now, yes-!! -M

Subject: Re: Singularity　　　　　　　*Tue Sep 16 2003*
To: Searcher　　　　　　　　　　　　*From: The Scribe*

Good afternoon Merrick!

I just finished the one and only case we have today and have the time and the desire to write without being tired or in a hurry.

I really do love reading your e-mails. And you still sound very young to me, maybe because you care so much in general...I am not sure! There is a zeal about you and a caring for the human race.

I will be as frank with you as I know how because if you want my opinion, I cannot tell you what you want to hear only. Some of what I say will seem naive, simplistic and probably unrealistic but it is a lifestyle and a belief.

Caring for the human race comes in many forms. You are a thinker and an educated man, a man of vision and of caring. Me, I am concerned about my neighbour and the woman who cleans the bathroom and the homeless man on the street. I cannot save the world, but I can work with what surrounds me and make life a little easier for the man next door.

As you said in your note, things are hurtling forward at a fast pace and I have watched this for years and many generations before have...all have come to the same thoughts that you did. Every generation has seen the progress they live with as the end of civilization as we know it or as they knew it. Technology is progressing, I can see it even within my work in the last 15 years and the changes we have made and the progress we have accomplished. People live longer not necessarily healthier or better. We throw defibrillators into people and shock them to live another few months of misery and we call it healthcare…emphasis on the care, how ironic!

I had mentioned before that the money that I make I use mostly for others. I said it maybe in a round about way, but that is how I have lived for years now. It is a small contribution to the suffering of some people who come in my life. Globally, I have very little vision and since there are inevitable happenings for the future, I have hope through my faith.

When we had the chance to destroy the virus of small pox, we did not. We chose to keep some of it for ….I do not have even a reason for it except what you had suggested before, the moral dilemma that we face constantly, the lack of caring and moral responsibility. We want more than we need! We need more than is necessary and hence we accumulate and horde. And to get more we use others and climb over their shoulders.

Yes, you are right! A few people can make so much difference in the lives of all the hungering people of the world…go figure!

One of my friends wanted to visit the Hearst Castle and I drove him down and was sick to my stomach for days at the decadence and the immorality of such a monstrosity during a time of depression and hunger. I am not a communist nor do I hate capitalism…actually I love living here in the States for that. But, there is no good reason for this blatant disregard for others and the complacency and the lack of empathy.

[Taking a breath and getting off my soap box.]
With lots of love,
Salma

Subject: Afternoon Blessings *Tue Sep 16 2003*
To: The Scribe *From: Searcher*

Good afternoon to you as well!

The big computer project I was going to work on today was shipped incorrectly. It's just as well. I'm a bit tired today & not feeling overly sharp. When this feeling is really strong, analog activity is always best for me.

>And you still sound very young to me<

you don't sound old to me. :-)

>some of what I say will seem naive, simplistic and probably unrealistic<

I don't believe this at all, and I don't judge feelings & expressions like this. However, if you'd stated something like this as fact: "all of these tech concerns will go away with personal force fields…" I heard those words this weekend; he was very young.

Women access different empathy pathways. I believe it's genetically based, and dates back thousands of years. This aspect is one of many I cherish within the feminine. Men usually wage battles of domination & scale within any given space; women see a village & individuals needing care within the same space. Don't apologize for this; celebrate it!

This empathy difference, more than anything else, is why I sent that long note to you. Your specific thoughts & feelings matter, and any comments you have will be additive to my experience.

>you are …an educated man<

Thank you, but this isn't true in any classic sense. I don't have a college education. Whatever it is I've "learned", it's been through my many experiences; one of which was being married for many years. If I were trying to describe myself, I'd say experienced, not educated.

Today, experienced enough to *not* be sailing this week. During my youth, I was different; having competed against those being overly decadent right now. Contemplation removes ignorance, keeps one young too, by removing conservative "mine-ness".

>People live longer not necessarily healthier or better. and we call it health care...<

When medical science doubles our physical life span or even quadruples it in the near future...I don't see this as progress.

You haven't mentioned if you have any children. I don't, but there was a short & interesting discussion about this phenomena during our roundtable dinner. Which genes are being perpetuated in the gene pool, and why?

>make life a little easier for the man next door.<

You're a beautiful woman Salma. The lives you touch are so blessed, and I for one, know the truth in this. Being a "man next door" to you is heaven on Earth.

Merrick

Subject: Re: Afternoon Blessings   *Tue Sep 16 2003*
To: Searcher   *From: The Scribe*

Hello my dear friend!

Thank you for that giving spirit of yours. you are a true testimony to open mindedness and vision. I am truly impressed.

But, do me a favour! Never describe yourself as not educated again...please! Education is not a degree and never has been and never will be. Education is learning! I am educated and being educated on a daily basis. My life is a long session of education and so is yours.

Yes, I do have children. Tracy is 24 and she is a Staff Sergeant and a Drill Instructor in the Marine Corps. Lillian is 23 and just graduated from Northeastern University in

Boston last September. Lillian lives with Tracy to take care of my grandson Tommy who is 5 now.

When Lillian calls me to ask me what to do with her nephew about certain things, I always throw it back to her. I always ask if whatever he did is going to affect his character in the future, is it something that will build him up and people around him or is he going to learn to be self-centered and egocentric with it. If it is trivial but will not affect those things then let it go but if it is trivial and that important then do something about it.

I raised my daughters on my knees. I was a single mom for many years and wanted the best to raise healthy intelligent strong women who can carry on and live without apology and without blame.... with open hearts and loving souls... non judgmental and kind.

I think I have succeeded. I am very proud of my daughters who are my friends. They know me inside/out and sideways, know every flaw and every crappy thought and every misconduct. :-)

Your new fan,
Salma

Subject: Mom, meaning, and a pillow   Tue Sep 16 2003
To: The Scribe   *From: Searcher*

Hello Mom! ! !

Wow. Your words set me aglow; a delightful testament to what's possible when an open heart merges with the Loving Essence.

I'm the oldest child, my little brother 8 years younger. Both parents worked; occasional diaper duty, and difficulties with alcoholic relatives, turned me away from becoming a parent. Today, looking back, I'm so grateful, even though little kids are usually fascinated by something they "see" in me.

>Education is not a degree

You and I are in complete agreement, however those within the towers of commerce believe otherwise. I didn't pick up a piece of paper along the path, so my journey's been challenging. No matter how it's turned out, I wouldn't recommend it. Each chapter has been its own strange script. Here's what happened, instead of a "higher" education:

18 - go to work, production job
promotions to top lead position
took a look around, asked "what's next"
supervisor said, no paper, no promotions
manager agreed it's the only way
VP agreed too, vowed to move on
3 months later, end of the line
25 - start another chapter
and so it's been since,
without BS, or any other alphabet soup

- * - * - * - * - * - * - * - * - * - * - * - *

Your original CL inquiry stated how you miss good conversation. To my way of reading this, there's an implied event that took place. If you don't mind my prying into your personal space, would you be okay expressing what happened?

On a lighter note, here's a heartfelt offer for possible consideration.

If you reach a point where you're comfortable enough with me, these days, I fix computers for a living. I'm not a

MS Windows fan, but I can certainly fix your VAIO if it's repairable. It's a no strings offer, one heart to another. However by doing so, it might become necessary to reveal more of yourself than you'd otherwise be comfortable with, which I completely understand. Reading between the lines, for all I know, having it working properly could be a laughable priority.

Is there anything else you'd like to ask?

As for me, I'm tired, needing rest, so it's off to my comfy pillow transporter.

Merrick

Subject: Re: Mom, meaning, and a pillow　　　Wed Sep 17 2003
To: Searcher　　　　　　　　　　　　　　　*From: The Scribe*

Good morning Merrick!

Our upbringing can certainly colour the decisions we make for our future. There is a healing process for all of us, there was for me. Life has never been easy but it has been a blast. I am the oldest of three girls, raised in Egypt. My father made sure that we had the best education and he placed us in a British school. He is an engineer and still works, he is 86. My work ethic comes from him directly; Also, kindness and compassion. He was a powerful man with a wonderful job and never once did I hear him berate someone weaker or lower in status than himself... remember, this is Egypt we are talking about, third world, where human life is meaningless and those "below" you could be crushed.

Meaningful conversation! Most of the people that I know go through life as if they are floating through it without opening their eyes... like a dream. Things are bad some days and things are good some days but they never open their eyes except for the times that are bad. That is when they have something to say and it is usually about how awful their life is and how tedious things are and how little they have.

I shared a townhouse with two young men when I first moved here through Craig's List. One of them was "helping" a friend of his and brought her to the home because she was out of money and out of a job. He mistreated her for three weeks. It was a constant battle in the house. I was sick and my disgust with his behaviour has not ended. I have seen a side of him that I can never seem to put behind me. I had to move.

I do not know who you are. I probably do not want to… sigh! I love people but sometimes I need some illusion. People are so harsh and unkind. I am not sure how you are but what you write is delightful and touching that side of you is enough because I can almost imagine that you are a nice guy…. I know… silly! I thought my roommate was a nice guy too.

Just to give you an image of what I look like… it is nice to put some kind of picture to the words. I am 5'7", 150#, grey eyes, brown curly hair with blonde highlights (not real, LOL) and I am very pale. My Russian Armenian heritage took over in the genetic pool. My father is dark and so are my daughters and their dad but not me. I have an athletic body but I could lose a few pounds around my waist. I am an apple like men.

Your offer to fix my VAIO even though you are obviously a Mac lover is kind. I think maybe we can do that over a cup of coffee when I get over the need to keep you distant.

Respectfully and with love,
Salma

Subject: Re: Mom, meaning, and a pillow   *Wed Sep 17 2003*
To: The Scribe   *From: Searcher*

>Respectfully and with love<

Thank you for this morning's greeting & good cheer. I'll reply more thoroughly later, when a moment arises - it's going to be a busy day for me.

For now, please know this note didn't run me off. If you wish, try again!

:-))))

More to follow, likely this evening after another bus ride...

Merrick

Subject: Re: HeartQuote: Understanding   Wed Sep 17 2003
To: The Scribe   *From: Searcher*

Hi Salma,

To give you a better idea of "me", here's something besides spam that routinely floats into my Inbox:

"Whether your role is to lead others or simply to lead yourself, acutely understanding what you are feeling and perceiving is the prerequisite to understanding what others think and feel."

— From Chaos to Coherence, Doc Childre and Bruce Cryer, HeartMath LLC

http://www.fromchaostocoherence.com

Enjoy,
Merrick

Opening Merrick's e-mail, the chatter box sat back looking at the words without reading them.

'This is a long e-mail,' she thought to herself. 'He is taking time to talk to me.'

Being a talker herself, she found this interesting, that someone else, could actually, talk more than she did.

Who was this man really? What was he like? Was he just like his words showed?

She wondered if her theories about meeting online, were really better, than meeting, face to face. Thinking that online communication was less intimidating for men, she always corresponded, on that premise.

Grinning, she started to read.

Subject: Re: The mirror reflects
To: The Scribe

Wed Sep 17 2003
From: Searcher

Good Evening Salma,

This will be short & sweet,
so grab a big warm mug or tall glass!
>Most of the people that I know go through life…like a dream. except for the times that are bad.<

30

Exactly. This is so true, it's almost frightening; I find it true of most people in general, not just those I know. For just a few days after the 9/11 tragedy, people had a different vision of life. I've been walking these financial district streets for some time, and I tell ya, it's so rare to find a shining beacon. Most have a better view of their shoe tops than the world around them. Actually looking up, recognizing they're passing someone & smiling; it's like they might vaporize into smoldering goo or something. They'd rather walk around fearful. Pure speculation; the shining beings are likely Aries - kiss them. ;-0

Leaning back in her chair, Salma stopped reading. The kettle on the stove whistled and pushing her chair back, she went to the kitchen to make a cup of Constant Comment. Holding her cup in both hands, she leaned against the sliding doors of the condo deck, overlooking the bay.

Life as she knew it was changing everyday. Things happened all the time, different, strange and kept her in wonder.

She brought her cup back with her to the desk in the nook and started to read again.

>He mistreated her for three weeks.<

Ack. Did I ever tell you how much I *dislike* male oppression? In a moment, you might hear what sounds like a broken record. Thankfully, there are times when I have the ability to make a difference.

Hearing of such suffering sends me running back into a cave. As a semi-male creature, I'm *certain* males cause more suffering than females. However, when I say this to some of my female friends, they usually try to tell me how "caused" suffering is an even 50/50 gender split. Looking around at the many data points, I can't see how this is possible. Among many other things, human males are more violent & greedy, which manifests directly in additional caused suffering, which makes me ill. Ack

Sitting back in her chair again, Salma picked up her now cooling tea and sipped at it, looking at the words. She was bewildered. A man with feeling and sensitivity. Imagine that! Reading on, she mused to herself.

>I do not know who you are.<

Ahhh, if you were a geek, you'd know a great deal. I've purposefully given you the ability to see where I work, my PO Box number, likely a personal phone number too. However, I know this isn't your realm, but just so you know, I'm not hiding from view.

>I love people but sometimes I need some illusion. I can almost imagine that you are a nice guy <

I'm as illusory as the clouds & the horizon in the distance, and yes, a detrimentally nice guy too. Let me illustrate with one small workplace bit of humanism, which most people on the planet would -never- have done.

When I hired my assistant, she was placed on "probationary" status by my boss, the COO. I could agree with his reasoning, so we went with it. 32 hours/no benefits. When this time period ended, I was certain of her abilities, and wanted her to stay on-board. So, I went to my boss to remove her probationary status, and make her a "real" employee with benefits. He balked, wanting to leave her at 32 hours & no benefits for another year-!!

I'd already anticipated this, and worked up the numbers in my head. I then questioned him at length about why he wanted to do this, and he finally admitted it was purely financial, having nothing to do with my assistant's performance. In that moment, I'd backed him into a corner & he didn't even know it.

As a salaried drone, I proposed making myself an 80% employee, which would free up 20% of my salary to give my assistant *all* the benefits of being an employee. My boss was visibly stunned, but called in the controller to verify my proposed accounting. The deal was struck, and she's an 80% employee like myself.

AND I told my assistant all of my plans before I met with the boss man. I wanted her to know I'm not a usual company suit, and was going to bat for her. I couldn't predict the outcome, but reassured her I would do everything in my power to make things right. After the deal was done, she told me how exceedingly grateful she was. One of the reasons she came to work here was the direct result of her previous employer having too many management changes & her ability to get benefits constantly being pushed aside.

Intuitively I knew this, and stepped up to the plate. Incredibly, my boss had some transformative process happen during all of this, especially given his previous position. He decided to give me a long overdue (almost 12 months late) review. In the end, my base salary was raised almost 10%, and I was put at 32 hours (80%). I work M-Th, and my assistant works Tu-Fri. In the end, the company saved a little money, and kept two employees. I don't have to commute through the Friday madness of Marin, and my assistant receives proper & just dignity. Salma, I endeavor to do what's right, even when it could be personally detrimental.

I'm far from being a saint, and have attempted to give you what my life feels like to me. If you want to know about warts, misdeeds, or how I've made a mess of things each & every day, don't hesitate to ask. I'm human, therefore, I screw up.

'Hmmm,' thought Salma. 'A man of honor? A humanitarian? A pain in the ass who talked too much?'

Wondering how much a person can reveal of themselves on paper, she was amazed at his capacity for rhetoric, if that is what it was.

She laughed at her silliness, then continued reading.

>I am an apple like men<

Wait just a minute there missy, not all men are apple shaped. I'm the exception that proves the rule! 6' 0" - 5' 11", depending on who's doing the measuring, and 175-180#; yep kinda tall & thin is a good visual of my outer form. Unless it's a sunny locale, most notice my blue eyes right away, and very real blondish with graying hair, which flows past my shoulders when it's not ponied up. I've been given an interesting expando forehead option too, which comes from the cue ball men on my mom's side of the family. My father's side has the hair & thin build. A little bit of this, a little bit of that - it's just a body with an untraceable lineage. My grandmother spent years tracing, and never determined her family's source. From her research, we may have been "original" Americans. It's likely impossible to tell, because to me, the water's already flowed beyond the bridge.

>I think maybe we can do that over a cup of coffee when I get over the need to keep you distant.<

You underestimate Microsoft's ability to make things easy. To fix messed up software component (A), one might need to replace (B), (C), and (D) - or worse, especially if a virus or spyware has made a mess of things.

Salma, keep me at a safe distance forever, if that's needed. I'll be okay with it. You said e-pal, and that's my only expectation. My VAIO offer had more to do with shipping anonymously somehow, not some weasel attempt at meeting you. If you haven't understood it yet, the last thing I'm about is sexual conquest. Don't get me wrong, my appetite is still quite, umm fiery, however, my values are clear when it comes to male patterns. The facts are, I should give you reason to pause.

Have you ever wondered what might happen when the Beloved's mirror returns a vanishing image…?

It's light years from certain, but you could be that scary to me.

I've actively spent time contemplating, "who am I", and "how shall I live". The answers aren't usually pretty. I believe you have some understanding in these areas too, which is why I find your being so interesting, and unnerving.

Finish your mug or glass, and put this to rest. I'm in no hurry to find out anything - other than maybe "what's next"….

With love & reassurance,
Merrick

Subject: Re: The mirror reflects   *Thu Sep 18 2003*
To: Searcher   *From: The Scribe*

Here's my telephone number;… I will get home in half an hour and should be up till 1030. If you wish to call, please do.

TELEPHONE CALL

Only from the heart
Can you touch the sky.

- Rumi

"Hello..."

"Allllo."

"Salma? This is Merrick."

His voice sounded surprised, as if her accent and strange greeting, were not expected.

"Yes, hello Merrick. How are you??"

"I'm fine. It's good to finally hear the voice behind the words."

"Yes, it is," she replied.

"How are things goin'?"

"I am doing well, work is great and things in general are just fine. How was your work today?"

"Tedious. There are three sets of long staircases to go up and down, everyday. And everyday, there's someone who's not happy with, where their computer system, is. And everyday, I pick up said piece of equipment and haul it up or down those stairs. I do get my exercise."

"I bet," she snickered, lightly

"Is it just me or are we having a hard time finding something to talk about?" he questioned.

Hearing laughter in his voice, Salma smiled to herself.

"Now that would be a true shame, since we talk forever

37

on e-mail. I always seem to have something to say to you."

"True," he answered.

Silence for a few seconds, what seemed like awkward silence.

"So, what do you think of us meeting sometime for a cup of coffee, or something?"

"I never intended for my ad to lead to a meeting …."

"Yes, yes I know. But after talking for this time, don't you feel that we could meet?"

"I guess. Hmmmm, I was not looking to date or anything."

"Yes, simple conversation, I understand."

Sitting in her living room, her rather bare simple living room that contained a futon and four throw pillows sitting against the opposite wall, Salma felt sleepy. She could see her bedroom from her seat, her other futon mattress lay on the floor beckoning.

She was tired and it was getting late. She was normally in bed by 10:00 PM at the latest and this was approaching the sleepy hour and she was ready. Looking at her bed longingly, she yawned. She was not bored with the conversation, she was just tired and sleepy.

And truth be told, she hated the telephone. An instrument to be used for messages and communication on a business level. That was her father's fault. He instilled that in her.

Merrick sounded, ummm, soft, somehow. But again, she chose the wrong men, always. Why not let the heavens do it this time.

What in the world was she thinking? This was not dating material.

"What do you sleep on?" she blurted, suddenly.

When he chuckled, she slapped her forehead.

'Now he is sure, I am making a pass at him …sheeesh! What is wrong with me! He will think that I am being suggestive,' she thought.

"What d'you mean what do I sleep on? A bed?? The sheets are beige with off white stripes. It is a queen size bed…." He trailed off.

"I'm sorry," she said, "I was looking at my bed and it is getting late and I sleep on a futon on the floor. Soooo, I just, asked."

"And I told you. It's comfortable."

Nodding her head and feeling stupid, he, seemed amused and friendly. He did not seem leering or disgusting.

Steering the conversation away from her blunder, she took another tack.

"What did you do today?"

"The usual, long trip from home to work on the bus, then work. I went to lunch outside. The weather was great. Then home on the bus and back here. The bus is a difficult ride most of the time.

"I look around me and there are so many people who are so oblivious of their surroundings. It seems that they live in a world of their own, unaware of anyone around them.

"I try and catch their eye and they always avoid me. It surprises me," he finished.

"The men or the women?"

"Both. But, I mostly try to engage the women. Who wants to talk to a bunch of crotchety men heading disgruntled to work?"

"Sounds like the women are in the same category; from what you tell me."

"The women are better, in general. They are usually too scared. I think that I scare women, most of the time."

"In what way?" she asked.

"I'm too friendly, too something, who knows?"

"I cannot imagine that they are scared, they may be avoiding you for their own personal reasons; of commitment or otherwise."

"Ah…most of the women in San Francisco won't give me the time of day. Most are wearing headphones and don't make eye contact. Young, uppity, curtain climbers with cloned corporate clothing. Fashion conscious, whether it suits them or not. If it is the two piece sweater, which I hate, or the pinstripe suit. Whatever is in, they're bound to wear. They keep their heads down and refuse to meet your eyes."

That sounded angry to her. She shifted in her seat, giving her response some thought.

"Yes, I do the same thing when I do not want to be bothered. That, or have a book. That is always a good deterrent."

"It sure is. When I'm anywhere, I notice that book as a sign of stay away," sounding, resigned.

"Smart move. Women will make eye contact, sometimes, but not mean it as an invitation."

She thought for a second, then, "I guess men cannot win this one," she laughed.

"No, we can't win. The messages are all mixed up."

"I start my mornings rather early, as you know. We had a full day at work."

Was she trying to end the conversation? Why could she not talk to this man. She chatted at him for long e-mails? This was getting nowhere. They both sounded strange, to her.

"Well, I guess I should get to bed. I have to wake up early."

How many times had she repeated that, anyway??

"Well, it was good to talk to you," he said.

"Yes, you too."

"You should think about lettin' me fix your computer at least."

"Yes, but that would require meeting so that I can give it to you," she smiled.

Remembering that they had discussed that in e-mail before, she did not elaborate.

"Goodnight," said Merrick, softly.

"Goodnight," answered Salma, quietly.

Sonia Rumzi

POUNCING KITTEN

Oh soul,
you worry too much.
You have seen your own strength.
You have seen your own beauty.
You have seen your golden wings.
Of anything less,
why do you worry?
You are in truth
the soul, of the soul, of the soul.

- Rumi

Subject: pouncing kitten   *Thu Sep 18 2003*
To: *The Scribe*   *From: Searcher*

Hello Salma,

It was a long ride in today, the diamond lane was zero assistance.

As for the phone call - I knew it! You're unraveling me like a kitten playing with a new giant bundle of yarn.

Laughing at the silliness; today, I'm not riding in a standard green & white bus. This is my virgin trip inside the one GGT bus with a giant gray whale design. From the inside the bowels of this great beast, nothing appears any different.

Humm, maybe the kitten's experience is similar; bat bat, flip, roll, see what I can make it do! Also, calling my cell phone during the day won't be highly rewarding, it's sitting on the counter. Head, check; limbs, check; well, I seem to be in working order, but don't count on it. Beware, thus far, more analog today than digital.

You asked many interesting questions last night, and it's a challenge to keep my overactive mental strangeness from playing with the many permutations. What kind of bed do I like?? Salma!!!! At least you didn't ask if I had penis envy too ...

To date, I've known several Aries women, but haven't been close to them. I know something of myself, so for this reason alone, there's plenty to be cautious of.

After speaking to you last night, I am curious about something. Beyond your femininity, you have an earthly grounded feeling. However, most everyone feels more grounded than I do! Gazing at your astrological birth chart might be fun.

My chart's filled with fire & air. When these elements are expressed through me, they're a passionate *and* combustible mixture. It's taken me a looooong time to figure this out, yet the qualities remain. Much of the time, more balance would be highly valuable to me, but it's so often unreachable.

The one good part about my insane commute is crossing the Golden Gate Bridge every day. The ocean horizon over the Pacific, and the glistening sun in the bay waters are so calming & peaceful. Plenty of water & trying to keep my feet on the ground are key ingredients, and with that, I'll zip up my fingers.

With love,

-M

Subject: Phone call   *Thu Sep 18 2003*
To: Searcher   *From: The Scribe*

Good morning Merrick!

You must be just about to get off the bus or still on it or maybe already there…:-)

It was good to talk to you last night.

Salma

Subject: psst, don't tell   *Thu Sep 18 2003*
To: The Scribe   *From: Searcher*

Hi Salma,

Here's another from the great Inbox mystery, but pssst, don't tell anyone - because it might make all the high tech stuff obsolete:

"When man is serene, the pulse of the heart flows and connects, just as pearls are joined together or like a string of red jade, then one can talk about a healthy heart."

— The Yellow Emperor's Canon of Internal Medicine, 2500 B.C.

>you must be just about to get off the bus<

Looking at the time stamps, not really. I was on an even later bus today. This entire week, my usual "schedule" has been thrown all out of whack. Snipping at the leaves would be easy enough, but getting to the roots becomes a long story. As the years have gone by, my fingers have grown tired of typing it.

If prodded, I could type - but I'd rather try my voice for a change. It's an 'underutilized' asset, errr, maybe liability.

Have a great one today!

-M

Subject: Did I shock you?   *Thu Sep 18 2003*
To: Searcher   *From: The Scribe*

LOL! You do make me laugh when I read your missives. You are so well written and so well "spoken". I find everything you say keeping me riveted to my computer to take in more.

I ask many things when I feel the need to have an image. My intentions were honourable honestly. I did want to know what you slept on since it was late at night and we were heading off to sleep and all I could think of was my warm bed and snuggling under the feather blanket / duvet.

So you were on the great whale today huh? Hmmmm! I was writing pretty early today since I finished my workout and brought my coffee in to work with me. I agree, the Golden Gate is beautiful and I try and cross it walking once a week, honestly. Love to do it!

>"As for the phone call - I knew it! You're unraveling me like a kitten playing with a new giant bundle of yarn."<

What a sweet thing to say!

Salma

Subject: Re: Did I shock you?   *Thu Sep 18 2003*
To: The Scribe   *From: Searcher*

She asks:

>"Did I shock you?"

It doesn't feel like "shock" per se, it was more like, mmmmm, how far down this particular path should I go on a first phone call? Waaay too much, and she could run for the hills - not enough, could result in humdrum blandness, not really me...

To shock me, you'd need to change your stripes this week, put on a nun's habit the following week, vanish for a spell without a peep, and then wonder why I'm acting strange.

>My intentions were honourable honestly.<

Your intentions certainly felt appropriate, but it was far from ordinary. The question wasn't something "mundane" like what's my favorite color, or tastes in music… no, it was "what do I sleep in / on". This is something I might ask, especially if there's any feeling like a consenting green light. Less than this has gotten me into hot water, so as a cautious male, I try to step gently.

With hindsight, and your desire for imagery, how about a graphical encounter with the missing pieces?

Make the bed using 100% cotton sateen sheets, with a high silky thread count, in alternating bands of tan & light. These big massage mittens are delightfully sensuous, like an all night kiss. Add a soft blanket or two for comfort, and a soft feather pillow to rest a weary head. Finally, strip off all the daily constraints of worry & clothing, allowing the magic gentleness to directly cradle every pore…

This is what ripped through my mind in that moment. I *wanted* to say what I was feeling at the time, but ohhh how I didn't dare! LOL

When I asked you about your personal gender experiences, it wasn't without good reason. Had you answered with "never gave it much thought", we wouldn't be where we are today. I wouldn't have shared with you in quite the same way. The ones I seek to play with have an intrinsic understanding of the world around them, and more importantly, their own internal experiences are semi-balanced as well.

>all I could think of was my warm bed and snuggling under the feather blanket / duvet.<

I was calling you from just such a place, but then as I understood from this weekend's conference, it's not the information that's important, but the waves & currents within it.

>>…unraveling me like a kitten playing…<<
>What a sweet thing to say!<
Au contraire; sure there's a playfulness to the image, but kittens have needle-like claws too. Have you ever gazed upon the images of Kali? She's a kitten, and males are advised to be careful, or be popped like a balloon.
-M

Subject: Re: Did I shock you?   *Thu Sep 18 2003*
To: Searcher   *From: The Scribe*

>To shock me, you'd need to change your stripes this week, put on a nun's habit the following week, vanish for a spell without a peep, and then wonder why I'm acting strange.<
Hey I can do that… easy…. lol!
>I was calling you from just such a place, but then as I understood from this weekend's conference, it's not the information that's important, but the waves & currents within it.<
Very true! And, I would not have given you my phone number if the green light was not on. But there is much to talk about yet.
Ahhhh yes… the kitten may have sharp little claws but you must really watch out for the tigress with the larger claws.
What are the best traits in a woman?
Affectionately,
Salma

Subject: Re: Traits!   *Fri Sep 19 2003*

To: The Scribe   *From: Searcher*

Good morning Salma,
Meooow!
>watch out for the tigress with the larger claws.<
now now…:-))
The impermanence of the physical is something I have faith in. If She shreds me, there's a spiritual lesson in the outer form's bleeding & dying lump. No fears, thus it be some form of insanity…!
To shock me, you'd need to
>Hey I can do that… easy…. lol!<
Birds of a feather have little doubt.
>I would not have given you my phone number if the green light was not on.<
Ouch! :-)) There's a challenge knowing your intelligence, and this mutual ability to leap ahead so easily. Caution says slow & gentle; my bold & rash, charging forward instincts are barely controllable.
>But there is much to talk about yet.<
Undoubtedly true as well!
>What are the best traits in a woman?<
Many things leap to my mind, your individual mileage may vary.
Disregarding for the moment, the mysterious beauty of the feminine form with it's inherent ability to create & nurture life, I find there's an important trait in energetic union. At least from the male side of the fence, male to male energy pairings lack the potency a woman can add. This isn't sexual, it's heart based wisdom & energy that's transmuted to the male. In my experience, other men can't do this for their gender.

Without doing the trans-gender shuffle, I can't prove this, but even the genetic code seems to indicate it's relevance. 0.5 (missing male leg) + 1.0 (complete female) = the appearance of two whole beings. From a male perspective, we'll do ***anything*** to experience this, stopping short of nothing in the quest. It's a position of weakness, and lends additional credence to the approaching age of male extinction.

Given the end of biological necessity, can woman flourish without man? I believe she already does this today, but often sees otherwise.... Can man flourish without woman? In my experience, I highly doubt it.

.02 cents worth of what I feel is best in a woman!
-M

Subject: Impulsive Illusion   *Fri Sep 19 2003*
To: The Scribe   *From: Searcher*

Dearest Sprite,

Today is a banner day for me, for I have fought off physical expression, well more or less anyway.

I didn't call last night, preferring some additional time to contemplate. I also wanted more beauty sleep, because ugly Merrick isn't a pretty thing. You didn't call either, and I find this equally fascinating.

During our call, you give me more than enough to act crazily.

Imagine today, a card arrives, proclaiming your deep humanness & undeniable zest. A rush of Spring's promise, among the harvest bounty. Consider this note, such a card - for it pains me to not deliver the physical form...

Ohhh, and it doesn't stop there either! Oh no... not me!

A giant bouquet of white roses arrives, arranged, delicate, stunning. If I thought those around you could cope, they'd be fiery red, aglow with celebration. This is what you've given me, and it's taken *considerable* effort to NOT make this happen.

Sitting here this morning, with a warm mug & freshly washed slumber, it's still a struggle. It would be sooo easy!

Putting you in a place of endless questioning would not be kind. I also know you work in a place where healing happens, so such a gift couldn't be wasted. My impulses scream do it, do it now. There's a smile at the end of the rainbow, an open heart to be touched...

Yes, affectionately.

Yes, with love.

Yes, thank you!

Merrick

Subject: Flattery   Fri Sep 19 2003
To: Searcher   From: The Scribe

Flattery usually gets you everywhere.... be cautious whom you flatter!

Yes, I have never been known for my wall-flower behaviour and it got me in trouble many times while living in Egypt as a teen. I was considered a hellion and really was not by any standards. They still remind me... sheeeesh!

It is true for men and for women my friend that there is a lack of completeness without the other.

Dante said that we all arrive on earth hermaphrodites and split as we touch earth, male and female. From then on we go our separate ways searching for that same half, looking for our soul mate for the rest of our life. Some of us meet and gel and mesh and some continue their quest for that complete. How sad!

I was trying to explain to one of the gentlemen that I

correspond with that I am quite unremarkable looking. He did not agree even though he has never seen me...:-) Imagination is a powerful thing. Anyhow, to prove my point, when he told me that he frequents Cafe Toronto on Bridgeway in Sausalito, I explained that I go there too and he has never talked to me. Which means one of two things, either that old fashioned approach has disappeared or I am invisible!

Being invisible has its merits... LOL! We walk through life everyday and never touch another person (not me)... I touch as much as I can... I hug my coworkers and my patients and my Boss and my Doc, everyone deserves 7 hugs a day...:-)

People say interesting things around me as if I do not listen. I hear so many things that I should not because I seem invisible to some. I like that!

Affectionately,
Salma

Subject: Touched   *Fri Sep 19 2003*
To: The Scribe   *From: Searcher*

>We walk through life everyday and never touch another person (not me)... I touch as much as I can...<

Oh Love, careful.

It's been hours since the power in this washed over me, with the tears drifting away in domestic chores. This example touches every fiber of my being; physically, emotionally, spiritually.

In your feminine form, you have the opportunity to give all of life's joyous treasures to others. The radiance you and I know of is available for your full expression. In this society, I can not.

This rips at my heart in ways I can't express in words.

Male physicality in the form of a hug, or even the less

"threatening" touch of a shoulder is so often unacceptable, except in many situations of sorrow & loss. This societal inability to fully share life's endless joy creates a crushing heartache within me.

Maybe I can share something of this; imagine every heartfelt moment where you've reached out to someone. Picture it clearly, the feelings you're conveying through your expressiveness.

With that firmly established, consider what it would feel like, if just before each & every one of these moments, a filter was put into place blocking the heart's action from happening.

This filter is real, and I'm not certain many women can understand what it is I'm trying to say. I pray women never lose the ability to openly share their experiences with everyone, because for some men, it's been a challenging loss.

I see this in action all the time. Women can approach others with ease; men hesitate, staying a comfortable handshake distance away. It's a filter that's completely unnatural, but I can assure you how real it is. All one has to do is read a bit, sexual harassment here, restraining order there,,, fear escalates, and society is caught in a really bad place.

While walking the streets of SF, if I were to touch men & women on the shoulder in equal numbers, it wouldn't take long for the authorities to stop me. In the average workplace, where there's some familiarity, doing the same would get me reprimanded, or worse...

For me, this is a challenging place. I feel, but expressing it so easily & openly isn't really possible. I pray women never ever lose this, for the world will be a sad sad place...

Ask a bunch of men how many strangers they've hugged in a month / year. Ask an equal number of women the same thing.

I'd be shocked if the numbers were balanced.

Yearningly,

Merrick

Subject: Re: Touched   *Fri Sep 19 2003*
To: Searcher   *From: The Scribe*

Hello Touched Merrick!

:-)

Yes, actually I do understand what you are saying. Women in the US actually do not like men…or it seems like they do not. Maybe it is that they just do not like men except the ones whom they can benefit from. They seem to have an adversarial relationship. How sad!

Women like me genuinely like men. It comes from my father whom I adore. He is 5'4", intelligent hazel eyes and a kind and compassionate heart. He was very powerful in the government in Egypt and yet treated people with dignity and respect. He never abused or took advantage of his power and money.

Yes, it is easier for me to touch others and to hug and kiss freely and much harder for you and men in general. It is rather sad.

We say in the lab that harassment is graded not reportable. One of my coworkers burst out yesterday and said:" Salma, I am so glad you moved to America." He likes that I am not pc, not uptight and not about to report every little nuance and word we say in the lab. I am who I am and I say many outrageous things, you know that! Not meaning to really. I just do.

I promise not to get an order of protection against you… hehehehe! I think I can take care of myself.

Lovingly,
Salma

Subject: Re: Impulsive Illusion   *Fri Sep 19 2003*
To: Searcher   *From: The Scribe*

Hello Ugly face!

Thank you for the sweet, kind sentiments. Just the thought is enough! You made my afternoon.

I did not call because I like to give men lots of space.. an American tradition of spaceness. I want you to feel no pressure to call or not call, be here or not, write or not. I will respond to whatever you put out there in your own time. I have the option of holding back or responding so I also have choices.

All is alright!
Salma

MEETING

*Out beyond ideas of wrongdoing and rightdoing,
there is a field. I will meet you there.*
-*Rumi*

As a morning person, sunrise was her friend. She never spent time in the sun, but she basked in the warmth and the light, without direct contact.

Feeling elated and energized by the good weather, Salma got ready to go for a walk across the Golden Gate Bridge.

It was a glorious morning, with the sun sparkling, on the water. Since the weather was crisp, yet warm, she wore red lycra gym shorts and sports bra, a grey t-shirt over it, socks and sneakers. Her earphones with good techno, bouncing music went on next.

Stopping at the doorway, she turned back, then picked up the phone.

Dialing his number, she waited for him, to pick up.

"Hello, Salma" said Merrick, recognizing her number and phone ID. "Good morning."

This was the Saturday, right after their Thursday phone conversation, where she humiliated herself.

"Hello Merrick. Would you like to go for a walk? I cross the Golden Gate Bridge almost every weekend since I moved here and I was wondering if you would like to come and take a walk with me," she said, without taking a breath.

Silence.

There was no sound on the other end for a few seconds

longer than usual. It was the silence born of doubt.

Then, he said, " Listen, I have to hop in the shower, get cleaned up, and get there, and, that should take me about an hour."

"An hour?? Where do you live?"

"I live in Sonoma, about 45 minutes to an hour from you…"

"Wow! It's alright…"

"No, no. I will be there, but not, in time. You go and walk and I will meet you there."

"I will be wearing my earphones that you hate so much," she said, chuckling. "I like to listen to music when I walk, alone."

"Of course," he said, laughing. "Remember, I am the skinny, tall, geeky computer dude, with long hair, blue eyes and Tevas.

"I am 5'7", plain, shoulder length brown hair and 155 lbs."

"OK. Sounds good."

"Okay, bye. See you soon."

After they hung up, she went to her car and drove down Bridgeway to the lookout on the North side of the Golden Gate Bridge, Vista Point. Parking, she set the earphones on her head, then walked to the bridge.

It was a glorious morning. The weather in September was perfect in San Francisco, especially on the North side. She smiled remembering what she had read a few weeks earlier, "God made the world for everyone, and Marin, for Himself."

'How true,' she thought.

Everything about Marin was beautiful. The hills were curvaceous and when the fog rolled down them, towards the bay, there was no way to express the beauty and majesty, of the design and haunting appearance.

High stepping fast and steady, feeling elated and happy, the walker, realized how fortunate she was, to live here. She loved being here. Having dreamt of this for fifteen years, Salma, finally lived in Sausalito. How amazing was all this.

Arriving across the bridge to the South side, she was moving fast and strong. Turning around, she walked back towards the North tower, returning to her car.

People were waking up. Several guys passed her, as she walked north, none seemed like they would be him. At least, she hoped, none of them were him. She smiled at her shallowness.

As she approached the North tower, she noticed coming the other way, a handsome man with severely cut hair, pulled away from his face, sunglasses, blue shorts and sandals.

Looking at him, he did not look back, but kept walking. After passing each other, and a few strides, she turned around to look, just as, he was turning around to look, also.

Looking at each other, they burst out laughing. Leaning her elbow on the railing and laughing out loud, she recognized the short treachery. His face was lit up with joy.

Moving towards each other, it felt that they had done this, many times before. Salma, the wanderer, walked right into his arms. They hugged, close. They kissed, a simple, quick, delicious kiss, feeling, soft lips. Laughter was the only sound from them.

As they turned around, Merrick reached out and took her hand. Salma was floored. He did not need to take her hand, really. She looked up at him.

"That was funny," she said.

Turning around, he showed her what he had done to his hair. He had pulled it back with a rubber band. Unless you looked behind him, you could not see the pony tail. Also, wearing sunglasses, so unless he took them off, you could not see his blue eyes.

"I drove across the bridge; I was pretty sure which one you were."

"Yeah?" she asked.

"Yeah. You seemed happy, ponytail and all," he said, smiling, running his hand over her hair.

When they reached their cars, he took off his glasses and she could see his clear blue, intense eyes. Putting his hands around her neck, he pulled her close to him, kissing her, fully on the mouth.

Kissing him back with abandon, she reveled in his touch. They hugged once more. This was no duck-hug. This was, a full on, body contact hug. They did not lean their shoulders into each other, to make sure their bodies, did not touch. They stood knee to knee, chest to chest and arms around each other, for a full body hug.

"So, where should we go?" he asked.

"There is a small café in Sausalito called Café Toronto. We could go there. They have decent coffee, and tea."

"I'll follow you," he said.

Driving down towards Sausalito, both thinking of what a great meeting this was, already, they were expectant.

She was scared because she had not planned this. He was scared because it all seemed right.

Arriving on Bridgeway to Toronto Cafe, they parked their cars. Salma noted that Merrick drove a van. Wondering what that could tell her about him, she mused at her thoughts.

She waited for him as he approached her, taking her hand, again. Smiling, she looked down at their hands. Amazing.

Sitting on the bench near the side door, she, against the

wall, and Merrick with one knee up against her thigh, she looked at him closely. He took his sandals off.

'So, those are Tevas,' she thought.

An East Coast woman was not sure what Tevas were, and now she knew.

She looked at his feet. She kept glancing at his feet. He had nice, long, clean, well groomed and not so soft, feet. His ankles were thick and solid. She dragged her eyes away.

Finally, she took a good look at his face. He had angular lines, a soft jaw and clear blue eyes. His hairline was receding. Blonde and graying, his hair was cut closely on the sides and left down below his shoulders in the back.

His mouth was full but the lips were thin, over perfectly cut teeth. No caps for this boy, all natural and the flaws were endearing, as few as they were.

'Workman's hands,' she noted. 'Sturdy.'

He had long fingers and solid nails.

Being long and thin, he was not skinny, he was lean, not muscular, but firm.

He kept his hands on her as they talked. She kept her smile and hands on him.

When he spoke, she was surprised, at the softness in his voice.

"Things are hard these days," he began, quietly. "I'm going through some things in my life and I'm not sure where they're heading."

"We all go through things in our lives and we do not know where they are heading."

"I have been divorced for five years," he said. "I live with my x-wife."

"Wow! That's amicable," she quipped.

"I moved out and could not afford it, financially. We

talked and I decided to move back in."

Should she ask the extent of the relationship? He did not offer. She learned a long time ago, not to pry. People will tell you what they want to tell you. Invasion causes distancing.

Their talk came easily, their connection, comfortable. How scary. How wonderful. How frightening. How incredible. How alarming.

The Jasmine tea, they ordered was cooling, as they talked. It's aroma was delightful. Nothing seemed to invade the calm. No one outside the two of them, existed.

If you asked them, they could not remember what they talked about, sitting there, so closely. They could remember how it felt, how close they were, the proximity of the other, but not what they said, in that hour.

"Would you like to come and see my apartment?" she said, suddenly.

He looked at her uncertainly, then said, "Sure."

Why did this not feel weird? Why was asking a man back to her apartment, after knowing him for an hour, not feel strange?

Live dangerously.

What if he killed her? Was that how women got in trouble and died!

Arriving at her apartment, he looked around him, and smiled.

"Bare minimum," he noted.

She nodded.

Walking through her small space, he felt safe and comfortable.

Entering through the archway to the bedroom, he looked at the futon mattress, on the floor, pointing at it.

"The famous futon," he started, "that triggered the

interesting question."

"Infamous was more like it," she scorned, herself.

Her bathroom was well lit, spacious and bare.

Walking back to the sparse living room, he sat down looking at her.

"I really like those pillows," he said, quietly, pointing at her large floor pillows.

She nodded.

Kneeling before him, he pulled her close between his legs as they kissed, long, slow and conscious.

Tugging at his shorts, he helped her pull them off. And she tasted him, for the first time.

He did not get hard... not very hard, really. She was wondering what was going on. None of it added up. He seemed shell shocked, well, who would not be? They just met, and here he was with her in her apartment, and they were having sex, and she was expecting him to what?? Perform??

He did not seem embarrassed or self conscious about it, he just seemed excited and reserved all at the same time. She coaxed, caressed, loved and touched.

Nervously, happily, they kissed and touched.. They were silly and childlike. He touched tentatively, touched with care and gentleness. She wanted to push and instinctively knew not to, he wanted to go slow. He was discovering and she was barreling into it.

Salma enjoyed rough and tumble. Merrick was slow to the rise.

He set the pace and she reluctantly acquiesced. He was stunned and dazed. Sitting back on her heels, she watched him. He looked down at her, and smiled, tentatively.

"Where did you come from?" he whispered.

"Egypt," she rejoined, saucily.

Crawling back into his arms, he held her, against his chest. She could hear his heart hammering, against her ear. He held her tightly and she burrowed into him.

"Will you stay for dinner?" she asked.

"I have some things to take care of at home. I need to make sure the pets are taken care of, but I would like to come back tonight."

"That would be great," she smiled, up at him. "Will you really come back tonight?"

"Yes, I really will come back tonight."

As he got dressed, she watched quietly.

Her mind raced. He could walk out, and she would never see him again. He could walk out, and she would have had just a few good hours with him. He could walk out, and she would never hear from him again. She would not be surprised, she would just be regretful, and sad.

It seemed that he could see that look on her face and pulled her towards him, kissing her gently while whispering, "I promise, I will be back tonight."

Walking to the door, he hugged her closely, patting her cheek, "Where did you come from?" he said, quietly, again.

She kissed his hand as he turned on his heels, walked down the stairs, out of her sight. She ran to the balcony and could see him emerge from the building. He looked up, she waved as he smiled.

Getting in his car, Merrick waved, blowing her a kiss.

His car took the turn, disappearing around the corner, giving Salma, as she walked back in, a feeling of great loss.

FIRST NIGHT

Let the beauty of what you love be what you do.
-Rumi

It had slipped her mind. Salma did not warn Merrick that, her only two friends, since she came to live in California, were coming to dinner, that night.

When she started riding a mountain bike, Salma met Melvin. They joined the same group of riders. On the weekends, they rode through Marin County roads, enjoying the exercise, the hilly countryside, offered. Melvin was in his late fifties; and single still. An accident got him laid off at his job and he seemed depressed most of the time.

As a drug company representative, Jamie came to Salma's work place. That was where that friendship started. It seemed to work. Both women had very little in common, but they got along, easily. Jamie was also alone, but active in the single scene.

It was Jamie's birthday and Salma promised to cook, so, she invited the only two people she knew.

Explaining to them about her meeting with Merrick that evening, they both listened, without comment. Internet dating was still foreign. It seemed to remain foreign, to most.

After a few glasses of wine and what seemed like an eternity to Salma, Merrick came back.

Meeting him at the door, they hugged, intimately.

"I forgot to tell you that I have two friends coming to dinner today. Sorry! Promised to cook for a birthday. I am considered a good cook," she tried, to explain.

Slipping her hand in his, she led him inside, to where her friends were sitting. She introduced them.

"Jamie, Melvin, this is Merrick. Merrick, these are, my only friends in California."

Handling himself really well, Merrick was not a little surprised. They shook hands and sat down to eat.

Not having a formal dining area, each person helped themselves and took a plate to the deck, placing it on their lap.

Cooking, being one of her passions, she made elaborate dinners. That spread, was Chicken Cordon Blue over rice, Quiche Lorraine and stuffed mushrooms. Arugla salad with homemade dressing topped off the meal.

Salma noticed, that Merrick, hardly touched his food.

Later, she found out that since he did not eat cheese, which was in every dish, and did not eat ham, which was in the chicken, and did not eat mushrooms, just on principle, he ate very little.

The conversation was not strained, there was much to ask and much to disclose. Watching him with her friends, she noted that, he was not nervous. He was at ease; relaxed.

He disclosed very little.

Answering questions directed at him, Merrick's voice was soft and low. She leaned into him to hear. He had fiercely, piercing eyes, alert and scanning. She watched him, as much as her friends did. He was friendly and reserved.

Excusing themselves tactfully, Melvin and Jamie, said their goodbyes, leaving earlier than anticipated.

All the windows and the sliding doors were wide open.

The beauty of this apartment was that the whole side, facing the bay, was glass. Sliding doors from top to bottom, floor to ceiling. The lower part of the window was also glass.

A full moon was shining, on the bay, and the night, was warm.

Left alone, to themselves, Merrick seemed trapped. He looked around him a few times, wondering what to do next. She smiled to put him at ease, and that did not work.

She felt like a barracuda. Most men wanted sex ....

soooo ...? What was the problem?? She smiled to herself. A rare breed?

Sidling up to him, she took his hand and led him gently to the deck. They watched the shimmering water quietly.

"Are you alright?" she asked, finally.

Looking at her, his eyes were shining with tears.

"I'm fine," he said, with feeling. "I am just surprised by how comfortable, I feel."

"That is not a bad thing, is it?"

"Not a bad thing," he said, sadly. "I haven't felt this peaceful in a long time."

Salma reached over and touched his arm to comfort him.

He took her hand in his and stood up, pulling her up with him. Moving towards each other, they kissed, tentatively.

Salma took his hand and walked inside.

He followed as though the inevitable was happening; as if he had no recourse, no alternative, no options, no resort...

"Are you alright?" she asked, hesitantly.

"Yes, I'm fine," he smiled, weakly, sounding nervous.

Undressing him slowly, she devoured, with her eyes, the parts of his skin, that came into view. An intake of breath, made her realize, that he was sensitive, to touch. Reaching for her, Merrick helped her out of, her dress. Naked for the first time, before each other, they looked on, in awe.

Suddenly, to break the spell, Salma started to laugh.

"This is all there is," she said, and stood up twirling. "No great show. Just an old woman."

Pulling her close to him, he kissed, her laughing mouth. She kissed him back and they pulled the duvet back and lay down on the futon.

They stayed close, facing each other while kissing.

Intimately touching him, Salma noticed the same response, from earlier that morning, limp, acceptance. He got hard enough to be inside her. No earth shaking love making here, just closeness. She held him, protectively.

This was a beautiful man. She reveled in his body and touched everywhere. She enjoyed his wispy hair. Muscular legs covered with soft hair, his arms were hairy, he was hairy all over, and she loved it.

She inhaled at his skin, basking in the thrilling scent. He smelled clean, not, soap clean, just, skin clean, just showered, clean. Burying her face in his chest, she inhaled, deeply.

He looked down at her, surprised.

"I like the way you smell," she said, laughing. "Is that weird?"

"No," he said, but did not mean it, she thought.

Making love to him, the love sick woman, adored his body and felt genuine affection for him. She could hear him gasp at every touch and her hands and tongue explored this new terrain.

'Whom did this man make love to? What were his experiences?'

Whatever she did, seemed to elicit a reaction from him, which encouraged her, to explore further. But, he did not get hard. He was semi erect, at half mast.

As the night came to a close, they were both tired and spent by emotion. They lay side by side, feeling sated and fulfilled. She had had better sex, but not, better company.

Sonia Rumzi

NEAR DEATH

Something opens our wings. Something makes boredom and hurt disappear. Someone fills the cup in front of us: We taste only sacredness.
- Rumi

Nightingales are put in cages because their songs give pleasure. Whoever heard of keeping a crow?
- Rumi

Subject: Suspended Thought   *Sun Sep 21 2003*
To: The Scribe   *From: Searcher*

I'm forwarding an old note for more understanding:
Subject: Suspended Thought   *Sat Aug 10 2002*
From: Searcher

Dearest Sangha,
Sadly, we never know how blessed our lives truly are until something happens. I've been traveling at higher freeway speeds for the last 8 days, averaging about 3 hours of driving per day. I noticed an unusual symptom last night, while pulling from a parking lot. I spent "too brief" a time this morning investigating it, not thinking too much of it. I felt I needed to be on time again, so I left for Oakland to hear the teachings of Jetsunma Kusho. Everything seemed as it's always been, the symptom no worse, and no better. At these low speeds (parking lots), my car wasn't turning quite the same.

Expressing the steering system failure is easy, but not the feeling I have sitting beside the freeway right now. Having stopped for a moment to purchase something, I began accelerating onto the freeway yet again. With a loud bang, the part broke, causing a suspension part to gouge into the left front wheel. The effect was to instantly lose some steering control, and a severe braking action was applied to one wheel. This human body is fine - the car, broken & immobile.

The feeling is beyond thoughts, words. The undeniable precious quality of our human embodiment is so sweet. Taste it, drink it, become so drunk, the awareness never allows your return to ordinary thought. The moment you have right now is all you have.

I was fortunate today. Had this happened during one of the many moments I've been traveling at 70 miles per hour, I wouldn't be writing this so easily. My life has been blessed yet again, and as before, tears of joy fill my heart...

Yes, I'll be "late" for today's oral instruction. It does not matter, I was on time once again as my heart received the teaching.

Blessed with Love,
Merrick
OM AH HUM HA HO HRIH

Subject: Re: Suspended Thought   *Mon Sep 22 2003*
To: Searcher   *From: The Scribe*

There are no words to express my joy that you were spared so we could meet.

Your loving,
Salma

"You bought a microwave?" he said, as he walked into the apartment.

"I did. I realized that you needed to heat your tea. You know," she said, playfully.

"Wow! You set the clock on it, and everything."

"Huh? Set the clock? Of course I set the clock. It is not that hard…"

Merrick interrupted her.

"Before you get all huffy. It was compliment. Most of the women I knew waited for me to set up the clock on the microwave or VCR or whatever."

"I am a tech," she said, matter of factly.

"I know you are a tech. You are definitely a tech."

Then gently he turned and said, "Toni could not do it. I have lived with that all my life."

"Does that mean you will feel less wanted or needed since I do not need you to do those kinds of things for me?"

"Not a chance," he said, as he grabbed her in a bear hug.

"I can even change my own light bulbs and the oil in my car," she said, playfully.

Walking to the futon, Salma sat down and leaned back in the seat.

Kneeling by her side, he bent over, and kissed her. This, he did freely, and frequently, when together. He touched her constantly, reaching for her, many times, and often.

She responded, in kind. She touched, felt and explored. She hugged him, constantly, kissing his cheek, every chance she got. He responded, by closing his eyes and smiling. She loved to touch his hair. She petted him.

Noticing that he had something hiding behind his back, she watched, as he pulled it out, to show her. It was a spiraled piece of aluminum metal. She looked confused.

"This came from my near accident," he said. "My car, by some miracle did not just spin out of control. When I stopped by the side of the road, and got the car towed to a garage, that is what we found. This is a piece of magic to continue life."

Taking the foot and half long metal from him, Salma got a hook and hung it over the window. It spun in the wind freely, as a reminder to be thankful, for every day, they have been given, to be together.

She hugged him.

"I am so glad you have been spared."

When he closed his eyes, Salma kissed his eyelids.

"I am so appreciative that I have been given the opportunity to know you, and to love you."

They lay down. He loomed over her kissing and touching. She responded with ardor, as they ripped each other's clothes off.

Merrick seemed relaxed and content. He seemed more comfortable, making their lovemaking insistent, and fulfilling, to both. No more was he, shy or shocked.

He was a man, in need, taking, what he wanted. She was a woman, wanting, what he was ready to give.

They dissolved into each other's arms. It was a tumble and weave. Their arms and legs intertwined, fell apart and came together quickly, and relentlessly.

When he was spent, he fell over, exhausted, holding her, in his arms.

Surprised by his attention, she kept her hands, to herself. Over the years, she learned, that men love their "space" after lovemaking. Most wanted to be left alone, untouched. Merrick was different. He wanted the closeness, the nearness, the touching. She tried to keep her distance, but he pulled her closer.

She was falling in love. He was falling in love. It seemed like the whole world, should just, go away, allowing them to live their life, without turmoil.

He did not seem to hold back, anymore. There was an honesty to his lovemaking, a sincere desire that he allowed release finally, out of himself. He seemed, to her, more in abandon. His control and reserve were down, while he decided to enjoy himself. He did not seem as suspicious as he was.

She touched him, carefully.

"I knew something was not quite right, the first time around," she said, laughing, into his shoulder.

"What does that mean?" he said, laughing with her.

"It must have been atrophy or something. I knew that that shrivel, did not quite match the hands or the feet."

Rolling away from him, while he reached for her, she barely, got out of his arm's reach.

"I'll give you a spanking for that," he threatened. "I can't believe you just said that to me. Are you suggesting that I'm small?"

She was laughing too hard to get away fast enough, and he was upon her, holding her, face down, over his knees

FEELING

When I am with you, we stay up all night.
When you're not here, I can't go to sleep.
Praise God for those two insomnias!
And the difference between them.

- Rumi

-Observe the wonders as they occur around you.
Don't claim them. Feel the artistry moving through
and be silent.

- Rumi

Subject: I feel.....   *Sun Sep 21 2003*
To: Searcher   *From: The Scribe*

you left me feeling!
Yours,
Salma

Subject: Re: I feel.....   *Sun Sep 21 2003*
To: The Scribe   *From: Searcher*

Dearest One,
>you left me feeling!
Those three "often overused" words, which I consciously
chose for you to hear, convey the life changing experience
you've graced me with.

I wanted you to understand the significance our day had

on me, because I know dire things can happen within this physical realm. Better said, than left unsaid.

It's heart wrenching to be here right now, with you there. It's getting late, with the movie doing a fabulous job of changing the mental context for my upcoming contemplation.

I got a chance to live for a day. Another layer to my ignorance was washed away; what am I going to do about it? How will I live the rest of my days?

No longer the wider with love;
it's personal & focused, yes,
I do love you,
Merrick

Subject: Re: I feel.....   *Mon Sep 22 2003*
To: Searcher   *From: The Scribe*

Merrick...

Yes, better said than not said! I have to share with you what has happened in the last few hours since you left. I went from anticipation, to heartache, to loss, to pain and back full circle but the pain still remains.

I had to think of what I should do. I understand your situation and where you are at with Toni and that is not a huge issue in itself. But, I have to share some of my concerns with you so that I would not be holding back important thoughts, to me anyway.

I understand that you have a responsibility to pay off your debt but what I cannot understand is your need to "save" Toni from herself. You do not seem to realize that a woman who gets the attention that you give her does not understand divorce. You have not divorced her, my friend. Not in her mind! You also have not given her the opportunity to recover since you are there to pick up the pieces all the time.

People with addictions look for people who are enablers (another overused word) to save them and you have provided her with that. You take care of her pets, her plants, her home and her and visit her in the hospital… she is not living her life, you are living it for her. I know that sounds harsh but it is true and you have not allowed her to "survive".

Caring for your brother is different. He did not ask to be sick. Toni has a choice and she chooses to live like this. She will not recover until you leave her alone to fend for herself and her life. If she goes in the hospital, she needs to find someone to take care of her home and pets and plants… this way she will think before she decides to take a plunge. You have not allowed her to grow.

I found myself wondering if I want to live Toni's life, through you…. I have to live by Toni's choices, through you!

My choice is to do it for now because I absolutely and without reservation would prefer a part of you than none of you.

Salma

Subject: morning call!   *Mon Sep 22 2003*
To: The Scribe   *From: Searcher*

Hello Sweetness,

In my sore state, calling me this AM with a good laugh was pure torture - please don't stop! After our day & a mindless moment, I can fully appreciate why you don't get into many arguments with men. At the same time, these very same qualities pose an interesting challenge for me. This is quite good, for I thrive on such juiciness. Speaking of which, you taste divine! Given enough time & opportunity, you'll understand how much I *want* this from you. mmmm

mmmm mmmm

I've had this Post Office box for almost 15 years. Besides my parent's home, this has been the most stable part of "home" I've known. This tiny metal box in the middle of Sonoma has been a strange refuge. I'm slowly learning how to carry this with me, wherever I go. This is one of the reasons I was so instantly comfortable with you.

If you wish, I can also give you Toni's house information, but I'm relatively certain doing so wouldn't serve any real purpose. If you believe it's important in your life, I'll be happy to give it to you...

A quick follow-up, after showering & moving this AM, I felt really good. I sat almost motionless on the bus for an hour & a half, and Ohhh my God, walking... If I could stand here in the file server room for the rest of the day, heavenly. However, it's Monday, no assistant, and a four story building with NO elevator, other than my laughing thighs to move me about...

From one love filled heart to another,
-M

Subject: Re: morning call!　　　　　　　　Mon Sep 22 2003
To: The Scribe　　　　　　　　　　　　　　*From: Merrick*

>Really... you know me better than that by now...

I do know you better than this, however, reaching me is an important capability - which I wanted to make certain you've seen. This is a high practical issue, don't read into it anymore than is there...

I will not be leaving you alone & in the dark. If this is the way it's feeling, changes must happen. Much more later, for now, it's a busy Monday without assistance....

Merrick

Subject: Be kind!   *Mon Sep 22 2003*
To: Searcher   *From: The Scribe*

My sweetest man,

I give you myself as a lover. It is the only way I can reconcile myself with the situation. I do it freely so that I would have no expectation and so protect my heart. I will do it within your time and your want. Be kind!

A warning! If at some point I express that I cannot handle a situation, please take me seriously. If I cannot handle it for a while and I keep mentioning it, I will disappear. It is the only way I know how to do things. The only way I know how to deal with a hard situation is to remove myself from it. I just take myself away from the hurt. Get myself out of the situation that I cannot handle... forewarned is forearmed as they say...:-)

Yes, if you love me, you need to know that I adore you, every last little bit of you. I devoured your body that day to learn what I can of it. I learned some of what I wanted to know, the places I can pay attention to, the places I can tease, the places that please you, the sites that excite and torment... I can spend hours worshipping at the altar of your senses.

Subject: Re: Be kind!   *Mon Sep 22 2003*
To: The Scribe   *From: Searcher*

Dearest,

>...I express that I cannot handle a situation<

Salma, understand my vigilance to never cause you any harm - none is the only tolerable level to me. Causing damage & suffering to others isn't in my vocabulary, but as you can painfully see, my actions can cause the very thing I seek to not have happen.

This is why it's so very important for your honesty, intuition, and grace to guide you. Openly discussing the difficult is of utmost importance to me. I want to know every nuance that's bringing you difficulty.

>...I can spend hours worshipping at the altar of your senses.<

Please mark on your calendar the following date:

November 15, 2003

With the grace of God, this day is my treat to you. It's my belief you will enjoy this extravagant day, one in which our senses will be heightened. This is one experience of time & attention you might not give to yourself. I set this aside months ago, and for the longest time, I didn't know why...

Please, for me, mark your calendar with a big red kiss...

>I will do it within your time and your want. Be kind!<

You bring such joy to me, kindness is the only way to show my deepest appreciation...

Yours,

Merrick

Subject: Re: *MY* wake up call   *Mon Sep 22 2003*
To: The Scribe   *From: Searcher*

>Yes, better said than not said!

I thought so too, and with that, your note of such -great-importance. Please don't hold back on anything you have to say, I must hear it; your silence will not serve me, and ultimately us. I know there's a tiger beating in your chest, and how important it is to keep her from being caged up. So, my thoughts:

>the last few hours since you left... but the pain still remains.<

Yes, I know this. This pain & agony has been written all over my body, and is what you felt before our coffee shop adventure & my exposing where I'm at today. I fully believe your intuitions are sound, and encourage you to keep great trust in them.

>Toni has a choice and she chooses to live like this. I have to live by Toni's choices, through you! My choice is to do it for now.<

I'm so grateful for your open ability to act upon this choice, as you say it best, for now. The original inquiry was for email conversation. I've been open about my challenges, so it's apparent why I might seek simple email conversation. Going in with the first reply, I had NO intentions of meeting anytime soon, if ever. None of this was "supposed" to happen like this, LOL - at least not in my mind. My life **is** a mess, and given these circumstances, why would anyone wish to be near?

As a beginning step, even before that first reply to you, I'd emptied my storage unit, creating a pain in the ass reminder of the mess (making a tiny crack for the Universe, or as you did, new apartment space). I've been on a quest to simplify my "stuff". Without being ruthless & adding to the land fill troubles, I had a feeling it'd take me 4 months or so to clean up the majority of this physical stuff... that clock continues to tick, and is one reason I didn't call Tabby Susan (pet sitter) to remain within your arms yesterday. This "stuff" will need dealt with, one way or another. Here's another example. The flow of things recently forced me to handle the two differing 401(k) plans I've been a part of, which need moved & consolidated. I need to wade through this "legacy" crap, now more than ever. No matter what happens between the two of us, this process is vital for me to finish. I can't live without doing so.

This compromise with Toni, which I've freely allowed myself to be a part of *again*, is much too high a price. When we split this union, we were apart for almost a year, which she did well, even though we were seeing each other occasionally. I returned in a daily way & splat. I've been gone longer too, the seemingly inevitable results are now legendary. Speaking openly about this reveals the ongoing pattern, which is so apparent to you. Yes, I can be slooooooow to catch on.

Now she's in the hospital for probably the last time. If there's ever another episode like this, the legalities of it will befall those around her.

Toni's choice has been to live this way, and my "caring" has allowed me to be a part of that too. Unfortunately, my "caring" tumbles around, becoming a contributing factor in her troubles. I know this all too well, having sat in the cold hard Al-anon chairs until my butt fell off. This is one reason it's so small…

Now what?

With a fair size van & lots of sweat, I can pack it all up & remove myself rather quickly. I'm still dealing with the displeasing effects when I did this exact routine almost 5 years ago.

The flow of the river is allowing me to feel many things right now, the reason for so much to happen & going to the movie. For a moment, it was all cleared out, and what remains is the undeniable chain of bumps & kisses. If nothing happens by accident, then I'm one damn fortunate soul. I've been given a Universal wake up call…

Salma, in a week of leading beauty & one incredible day, you've changed my life. No matter how the river might cast me, there's a place in my heart for you.

This is why I can say, "I love you", in all its personal glory.

Merrick

Your openness and Your willingness to accept what I say so readily makes me tearful. I have to be careful what I say to you. You never fail to say the right thing to comfort me...I am getting spoilt.

Lovingly,
Salma

> My life **is** a mess, and given these circumstances, why would anyone wish to be near?<

Because you are who you are and because you are special in so many ways.

>and is one reason I didn't call Tabby Susan (pet sitter) to remain within your arms yesterday.<

I did not mean for you to call the pet sitter Merrick, I meant that Toni needs to take care of that herself... but you already know what I am saying and you understand it clearly.

The only reason things are apparent to me is because I have prayed since I spoke to you last night. It has been made very clear to me that I have to be with you for now... I am not sure how long or if there is a time limit but I always keep myself open.

Also, Toni is very clear to me because I am a woman and

I understand those controls and games. I refuse to play them but I understand them. Years ago God has taught me through some very hard lessons to let those walls down and be open and not use manipulation to get what I want. It is not an easy task for women. We are taught to manipulate to get what we want and I cannot do that. I am constantly being challenged by God to stay on the straight and narrow when it comes to that.

I am humbled that you share your life with me. I find myself wanting more of you just because of that. If I can be of any help let me know!

Your loving,
Salma

Subject: Unbounded Bliss   *Tue Sep 23 2003*
To: The Scribe   *From: Searcher*

Dearest One,

Given the state of "things", maybe I should have sought blessed orgasmic relief last night.

When things are going well on all levels, I sleep so soundly. When something's out of whack, it's not uncommon to be roused from sleep at -precisely- the 3:00 AM hour. I call it my sleep bandit.

Last night, I'd gone to sleep with a pillow between my knees; warm, comfortable, fully at peace. As the beautiful waking state began to emerge, I rolled over, the pillow providing a false sense of another beside me. I knew what time it was...

The ache from the earlier illusion of peacefulness became a painful reminder, the heart residing a false distance from joy. Scanning beyond the head & heart; throbbing, aching, a need to be touched, caressed, and held. I moved the pillow higher, placing my hand where yours would be & imagined once again all is right.

Damn it, it's not. This morning riding the bus, it's readily apparent how patience is NOT a strong point for me. Fine, I'll endure whatever it's going to take... to be caressed, held, at peace.

>I am not sure how long or if there is a time limit but I always keep myself open.<

The time we have together here in the Bay Area is so precious to me. Your life *must* remain beneficial to others, and I see this clearly. If the most beneficial & harmonious career path for you is starting up another new facility, then that is what's best. I'm not deluding myself into believing otherwise. This may not be available at this time too, which has different implications, especially given the desire by others to retain you.

I won't stop encouraging you to do what's best for others, brings the most harmony into motion, and increases the experience of Love in this manifested realm. This is who you are Salma, as the cherished manifestation of God.

As for me and my "career" objectives,,, years ago, I set out to create a career that's "portable". To some small degree I've succeeded. In many other ways, this work day stuff doesn't really matter, because I can do most anything I have a need to do.

What matters to me, is how relational difficulties are handled. When they've arisen in my past, I've tried to be there, to work through them, help create an environment for the rekindling of possibilities. Salma, I can assure you, this ability remains to this day. I pray no matter what happens, we'll retain our abilities, approaching life with our most honest & open Self.

>Your loving,<

Such heartfelt delight hasn't been felt in so long, and this time, there's a completely different, less "obvious" quality. When you spun around, laughed, and then so easily embraced & openly kissed a very strange man... Salma, something happened in that moment. It didn't feel like it came from me, and I was certainly unafraid to keep stepping closer.

Many months ago now, a former lover asked me "if I was happy with my choices". At the time, I wasn't convinced my path was leading me towards any greater sense of peace & joy. Breaking up from her wasn't nice, the yoga teacher training didn't turn out well, and then wham, knock me backwards onto my ass, the experience opens into unbounded conscious bliss...

Yes Salma, you may love me, and so much more!
Merrick
PS - stinkin' long bus ride, the thighs are still STIFF-!!

Subject: Re: Unbounded Bliss   *Tue Sep 23 2003*
To: Searcher   *From: The Scribe*

> As for me and my "career" objectives,,, years ago, I set out to create a career that's "portable".<

Dare I hope that you are mobile to a greater extent?? I am smiling all the time. I keep thinking of you and smiling like a cheshire cat...like I know something no one else knows... I do - you!

Awaiting to hold, caress, touch and love you,
Your Salma

Subject: Re: Unbounded Bliss   *Tue Sep 23 2003*
To: The Scribe   *From: Searcher*

>Dare I hope that you are mobile to a greater extent??
I'm not a shop keeper by conscious choice.

My career today is printed material related, which is world-wide.

Now my back on the other hand, has some mobility hindrances; but none you've found "too objectionable", at least not yet?

My brother called this AM, asking about Toni. He then asked me what I was going to do about the situation.

He then kindly, once again, volunteered his converted garage space. What a great idea!!! While laughing my ass off & thinking to myself, let me see: a three year old daughter, a five year old son, a cat, the wife, my brother & me... My wildest dream comes true!

>Awaiting to hold, caress, touch<

You're such a physical animal aren't you! sex, sex, sex, is that all women think about these days!!! Whatever happened to simple conversation???

>...and love you,
>Your Salma

Ohhh, I see, the conversation isn't bound up in vocabulary, as the Nitty Gritty appears with its Cheshire delight...:-)

Merrick

Subject: Re: Unbounded Bliss   *Tue Sep 23 2003*
To: Searcher   *From: The Scribe*

LOL!!

So, dare I hope that my humble abode seems a decent alternative to all this?? I guess there is a fight to have you near. Everyone wants you! Brother, former wife or adoring lover.... :-)

Salma

Sonia Rumzi

FLOWERS

Let the lover be disgraceful, crazy, absent-minded.
Someone sober will worry about events going badly.
Let the lover be.

- Rumi

Subject: Beautiful Server Room   *Tue Sep 23 2003*
To: The Scribe   *From: Searcher*

Mysterious Tigress,
    The strangest thing happened when I opened the file server room door. The onrushing cool air was carrying the most beautiful scent, much like the one I was recently so privileged to feast upon. Gazing, there's a clear glass vase in my favorite shape, filled with Spring's bounty; yellows & purples, reds & greens.
    If I were a sentimental romantic fool,
tears would be filling my vision.
    It's been soooo long since a stem was delivered to me, for simply being me.
    If I were a sentimental romantic fool,
these tears would flow into my heart,
further opening the unknown.
May I never get used to this feeling,
taking for granted the sacred gift of my Salma.
Sentimentally,
Merrick

Subject: Re: Unbounded Bliss   *Tue Sep 23 2003*
To: Searcher   *From: The Scribe*

My offer still stands... solid! I have the space and the need!

Salma

Subject: Re: Unbounded Bliss peppered with jealousy for Your time!   *Tue Sep 23 2003*
To: Searcher   *From: The Scribe*

Here is why they are yellow:

Yellow roses in the maturing form have come to symbolize the meaning of joy, happiness and friendship.

While this is true in the main there can also be suggestions or partial tones with sending yellow that are intended to bring in care or compassion, and these are subtle. In rare cases there may be allusions at jealousy though this is more the exception and a sensitive notion, to be sure.

Subject: mmmm, mmmm, mmmmmmmmmm *Wed Sep 24 2003*
To: The Scribe   *From: Searcher*

Most beautiful One,

Out of self protection, today is the skimpiest blue thong, caressing me where your lips had just been - containing what might be a juicy day.

I'm so bummed. To create a quick image for you, I reached for my antiquated digital camera. I was going to process the image while riding at the back of this bus, ultimately creating a link for you. However, it's been so long since it's last use, I'd completely forgotten how the camera is based on the old technology. It's going to take some effort to resolve this dilemma, but no worries, there's always a way.

While waiting here are some pictures for you:

http://www.fantasmagorik.com/

The image is from the time spent on my boat, dating back to the morning of October 04, 1998. It was the most incredible sunrise I've ever seen, and the picture merely scratches at the surface.

When you speak of "identity", which I wanted to ask you about last night - but for some strange reason the nerve fibers continued to be stimulated in other ways... God's glory reached out the morning this picture happened, stopping time, while the Sun continued to rise. When my life flows properly, it's like the morning this picture was taken & what you've experienced from my first reply. (White speedo image)

A project has come to mind, now I want your chart.

As precise as you can be, what time of day was it, and where were you born?

Blessings to those with an open heart, mind, and body!

Subject: Wow!   *Wed Sep 24 2003*
To: Searcher   *From: Scribe*

Good Morning my love!

I cannot describe my feelings this morning because they are too many to encapsulate in words... too profound to limit in letters and punctuation. But realizing what you desire has given me the opportunity to be who I really am and for that I am grateful.

I am grateful that you are going to allow me to live the way I need to. There is no love without a lover and no lover without someone to love. And here is the miracle... I had given up!

I do not know anything about the timing of my birth actually. That information was never given to me and if it has, it has never registered.... :-) sorry!

I cannot wait to see Your handsome face today. Yes, I am leaking, still leaking and will be I suppose all day…how perfectly wonderful!

Your loving,

Salma

Subject: Re: Limitations!   Wed Sep 24 2003
To: the Scribe   From: Searcher

My dearest Salma,

>It is so much easier to talk of those in e-mail.<

Hummmm, this statement seems easy enough to believe & understand, but if this relationship is to work, don't choose the *easy* over the difficult. This applies to not just limitations, but to all of communication. For now, this will certainly continue to work - but it's a crutch you shouldn't count on having.

Each of us in this manifestation are dead. We fully believe we're alive, but until we've escaped energetic recycling, death is. The enlightened beings that have visited this realm don't experience deja vu. The illusion of having already experienced something before has disappeared for them. They experience the past, present, and future as all knowing Reality. There is no illusion. If you're claiming full enlightenment, we celebrate.

Until then, everyone & everything within Maya is DEAD. This is not a hard or soft limitation, but the experience all of us live with at this very moment.

>Otherwise, I am not sure that there are things that you would ask me that I would not do for you.<

Something's already come to mind, which won't / can't be

spoken of until many many months have passed; so maybe you're not being clear, or simply naive to the vastness of what's possible?

With loving kindness,

-M

Subject: Re: Wow!   *Thu Sep 25 2003*
To: Scribe   *From: Searcher*

My sweet Salma,

You've been an unbelievably good influence.

I've yet to find a single incident on the Net where this moniker of your essence appears...??? This is such a good thing, it's like you've given it to me! :-)

Last night, we both knew it wasn't going to be easeful for me; I returned to find Toni barely functional. Convalescence & the return of anything resembling health no longer happen within the hospital environment. It seems the provided healing is only to the point of crisis mitigation.

This is fully understandable. Health isn't the removal of symptoms, but the gamut of life supportive rituals & routines. That being said, Toni's symptoms were removed, it's now up to her to find what it takes to become healthy.

As Salma looked at the words on the screen, her heart lurched in her chest. Realizing suddenly the impact those words could have on her new budding relationship.

This was not just her and Merrick. This was her, Merrick and one other person. A whole other person with needs, wants and desires that are probably contrary to her needs.

This, this other could be the one who impedes the evolvement of this marvelous relationship. What marvelous relationship? The one where he lived with Toni? The one where he saw her when he could?

When did she becomes the author of a character that did not exist? Who was this Merrick?

When did this becomes so intense? Harrowing was more like what she was feeling. This is not what she signed up for, was it? Why did she do this to herself?

How could things go badly so quickly. Something deep in her felt that this did not bode well. Something deep inside her shook. Heading for heartbreak was not what her ad implied.

The rules of the ad have changed with meeting. The rules she had set for herself had changed and she was the one who changed them.

No one was to blame. No one did anything wrong. No one lied. No one cheated. No one was deceitful.

She continued to read.

Sadly, the hospital didn't take one extra step for her (ultimately me) - which is a compassionate failing. They wrote her two prescriptions, but didn't call them in to her pharmacy. She was lead to believe (or fantasized) they were going to do this. So, in her exceedingly weak state, her medication was left completely to her. I think this is wrong. The staff should have taken the extra moments to do this.

As you can imagine, I arrived last night to find her waking from her rest - and - in her mind, figuring I could run over to the pharmacy & quickly pick up her prescriptions. I found out they needed to be filled, thus waited for them. I did this, along with picking up all the other things that she wanted, even though this wasn't what I needed for me. I was done about 9 PM, when I then gave myself the time to unwind. After a moment to eat something, the couch was a *perfect* option. I failed to keep enough energy in reserve so that I could drive to you.

Tonight will be different. No matter what happens today, I'm going to make sure there's enough in the tank to return to such a healthy place for me.

Onward, so you can see it in writing like this & hopefully gain some understanding too, for now, here's what I'm planning to do.

For the next few weeks, I'm going to be giving you approx. 1/2 of my available time. Some weeks there'll be more, and some there'll be less. If I were to go well beyond this right away, it would feel GREAT. However, after some careful consideration, doing so seems unrealistic, and likely hazardous for both of us. We have so many things to process, much to consider.

To this point, the time we've shared between us has been free & open. I want this feeling to continue, because that's where the joy & specialness of life resides. There will be plenty of time to work with life's more difficult moments together. I have no doubt about this. For now, I'd like to establish an *even* & solid foundation of mutual love and respect. To me, this is how we'll make it through where we are, to wherever we're going. Slowly processing whatever challenges present themselves is to our mutual benefit. Given a proper foundation, I don't see any reason why we can't build a joyous life together.

thoughts from a moving bus,

Merrick, your adoring
PS - please make up a key at your convenience, I want one.

Subject: Re: key!   *Thu Sep 25 2003*
To: The Scribe   *From: Searcher*

>you should see what happened to me when I read Your note about the key…guess?? <
A moment of sanity, causing you to run screaming from the room - clutching at your breast, gasping, wondering how you could possibly consider giving a madman the key to your peaceful sanctuary?
-M

Subject: Re: key!   *Thu Sep 25 2003*
To: The Scribe   *From: Searcher*

>I changed my pants once so far…the day is young yet.<
Restrain thyself woman, laundry staff will become equally desirous - further lowering overall company productivity.
-M

Subject: Day's Leap   *Fri Sep 26 2003*
To: The Scribe   *From: Searcher*

Wow!!!
What a day it's been. The steam-roller just keeps moving along, squashing everything in it's wake. First one minor thing, then another and another, until I look up at the clock & see that it's after 4:30 PM…
Had I not come today, my assistant would've been less than pleased. It was a good choice to work today, albeit, a

tiring one. It was a twinkle past 3 AM when my devouring lover made a similar choice, giving a smile to make it through this trying day!!! Because of your many gifts of love & heart, it's been a peace filled day.

Blessings,

-M

Subject: Re: Day's Leap   *Fri Sep 26 2003*
To: Scribe   *From: Searcher*

>I made the key this morning after you left!<
Will it let me out of this funny farm?
-M

THE DANCE

In your light I learn how to love.
In your beauty, how to make poems.
You dance inside my chest,
where no one sees you.

-Rumi

The fire crackled and spit. It glowed red, orange, yellow and surprisingly, blue. She mused as she watched it dancing.

Slipping on a black silk gown with thin straps, she felt sexy. It was transparent and the back dropped to the center of her behind. Tying a silver shawl around her hips, she moved in a circular motion watching herself in the mirror. She could see the effect her movement had, on her clothes, they shimmered.

Smiling at herself, she made faces, laughed, and covered her face; in shame, at her silliness. She made a serious face and frowned at herself, in the mirror. Critiquing what she saw, she approved of some, and squinted at others, sticking her tongue out, in disdain.

Strong, muscular and shapely legs, were a part of her, that, she liked. Her thighs were well cut and chiseled, the arch of her feet high, and her toes, polished in red. Silver rings, adorned the second toes, next to the big ones, plus, silver, ankle bracelets.

Holding her arms up, she wiggled them, nope, no flab

there either. She has not grown wings on her upper arms, yet. She smiled at the thought.

Noticing that the silver shawl stretched out, since, she had a bigger waist than she cared for, she shrugged.

'So, I am not, perfect,' she thought.

Being perfect had never been a goal for her. Even simple things like make up and hair spray were, of no interest to her.

Remembering her father's words as a teen, she frowned at herself.

'You have a superiority complex,' her father, had said. 'You think, you do not need any make up, or rollers, for your hair. You believe you look good, as you are.'

Wondering if he was right, she continued her examination of herself.

Turning to examine her behind, she approved of her compact and narrow butt.

She could always show her better side. She laughed out loud, at the silly thought, of trying to show only her backside, to Merrick.

Expecting him within the next hour, she was preparing a surprise, that might, please him. She slipped old fashioned, silk stockings on, making sure the lines on the back of her legs were straight. Smiling at the painstaking care she was giving this preparation, she enjoyed herself.

Curly, brown hair framed her face. Tossing her head left and right, enjoying the resulting effects, she looked on, with disdain. Yet, it brought the blonde highlights in her hair, which were applied on, to a glowing life.

Walking out to the living room, Salma lit all the candles she had in her apartment. They were strewn all over the floors, the doorways and the counters, the desk, beside the bed and bathroom.

The apartment glowed with eerie light. She looked around her and savored the sight. It was moody yet dark. It was mysterious as well as enticing.

She walked over to her little compact disk player and chose the music for her performance. A new age piece of music, that had Middle Eastern rhythms, that she could dance to. Playing it several times, she got the beat into her feet and body. Her arms moved sleek, over her head.

It was time for Merrick to arrive. She heard him at the door knocking then turning the knob, he entered. She disappeared in her bedroom.

He was met with shadowy darkness, flecked with flickering light; mixed to the smell of lavender in the air.

"Salma?" she heard him call, quietly.

"Please sit down," she called, back, "I will be right there."

The futon sighed with his weight, as he sat down.

Suddenly, the music started. Salma had set the timer on, as she heard him.

The music drifted to her senses, as she hid behind the wall of her bedroom, as she started her dance.

She moved her arms out, where Merrick could see, to the beat of the sensual music. Moving forward, she showed one leg and then came out, undulating and dancing, to the desert sounds. The music had a dreamy quality. Merrick caught sight of her, and she could hear his intake of breath.

He was smiling and his shiny, blue eyes were intent on her, watching her every step. The enticer, came closer to him, but just enough, out of his reach. She would come closer to him, then move away provocatively, just as he could touch her.

Dancing as if her life depended on it, she moved to please

him. She danced like a harem girl, who obeyed her instincts of survival and danced to please her owners.

Merrick was mesmerized. He was taken and abandoned where he wanted to remain, and not return. He was in a tent in the desert, he was a King, a Sultan and in control.

The music, the smells, the lights, transformed the mood. There was a sensual lift in the space. This was not "belly" dancing, this was "balady" dancing. The real thing. This was not exercise, this was a sexual, come hither dance. She did not sweat, she glistened.

Salma closed her eyes as she placed her hands behind her neck lifting her hair up, then languidly down around her shoulders, while moving her hips, in a circular motion, to the beat of the music.

Stepping one leg out and slowly following it with the other, nothing was hurried. Each was calculated to entice him, each step was designed to fill him with need and desire.

Not smiling anymore, but just staring at her, in that lust, that only this dance could bring about, the watcher was enthralled. The Dancer realized that her dance achieved the desired affect.

She quickly, looked away, like a shy maiden, caught in an unseemly act. Then she laughed out loudly, at her coy ploy.

The music was coming to an end. The dance was winding down. A five minute dance, that seemed to last forever. The notes were a lilt and a soft memory, as the song came to an end.

Quickly Salma went to the player, stopping it, before it could go on to the next song.

Merrick did not move from his seat. Keeping his eyes on her, as she came back to him, kneeling between his legs, he held her for a few moments.

"Where did you come from?" he asked, not for the first time.

"The aromatic, sweet sands of the desert," said the temptress, smiling, while resting her head against his chest.

"Where did you learn to dance like that?"

"Most Egyptian women can dance. They just do not. It is considered, unseemly."

"Unseemly?" he questioned, quietly. "It did not seem unseemly to me. It seemed unreal, like another world."

"Yes, it is from another world. It is from the times of seduction. Did I seduce you?"

"Ya, you did. You most certainly, did. Where did you get this music?"

"I have had it and loved it. I am glad I chose the right thing to please you."

"You please me more than you'll ever know, Salma. You've turned my life upside down. In the few weeks we have been together, I've experienced joys and pleasures beyond my imagination."

"Then your imagination is not wide enough. We have not started our life together, yet."

"You've expanded my imagination and stretched it to limits, that I didn't know existed, in this lifetime."

"This is our lifetime, and we have to do what we can, to make sure we live it, to its fullest."

"I find you enchanting; and full of life."

Not knowing what to say to that compliment, she smiled, quietly.

"Cat got your tongue? Did I say something that you can't answer, finally?"

He smiled holding her closer to him.

"You make me sound like a wise ass. Like I think, I know

everything."

"You do. You sure do, you minx."

The lights from the candles flickered around them, like diamonds. She could see the shadows on the walls. The light from the fire added to the magical quality of their surroundings.

"I want to stay here with you, and close the door on reality," he said, suddenly.

"Then we close the door on life. We are together in life. I am not going anywhere, and I am not letting you go away, either."

"Keep hold of me," he said, leaning, against her shoulder. "Keep reminding me. Keep holding on. I feel like I keep drifting away without anchor."

"We are together today, Merrick. That is all I ask of you, today. Don't be sad, today. Tomorrow is not here. Today is ours to hold."

He hugged her and laughed.

"Where did you learn to live like that, Salma?"

"Like what?" she asked, sincerely.

"You don't even know, do you? You don't know the power of the way you live your life. You live truly in the moment, and you don't even realize it."

Leaning back on her heels from her kneeling position, she was pensive.

"I suppose if I did realize what I was doing, that would be a forced realization of the way I am living," she said, seriously.

He nodded.

"I mean if you know what you are doing with your life, you are in an act, instead of a life," she said, smirking. "This is just me. There is nothing more or less. I have lived like this all my life. I am not even sure what you mean exactly, but this, is all there is to me."

He pulled her closely to him and closed his eyes.

There was not much more to say. His tears gathered and fell on her shoulder. She reached and wiped his eyes. Then taking his face in her hands, she placed kisses on his eyelids and mouth.

"You are not allowed to get away from me," she said, sincerely.

Merrick, laughed

BREAK UP

He is like a man using a candle to look for the sun"
- Rumi

-It may be that the satisfaction I need depends on my
going away, so that when I've gone and come back,
I'll find it at home.
-Rumi

Waiting for him to pick her up, she was in anticipation. They were going out this Sunday somewhere; he would not tell her. The weather was perfect Marin weather, balmy, warm, sunny, cool in the shade, with a breeze.

She waited. He did not come at the time, he had said he would. He came later. Looking pale and drawn, he arrived, around eleven thirty.

Sitting on the floor by the fireplace, she felt chilled.

He knelt before her, putting his palm on the center of her chest.

"Hello," she said, softly.

"Hello," he said.

He seemed to be holding back tears.

"I thought I should come and tell you, in person. This is not gonna work. I can't see you again," he croaked the words out.

With tears rolling down her face, she looked up at him. He touched her face, as she kissed his hand. She said nothing. She did not dissuade him. She did not ask why. She did not.

"I have to go," he said, turning away, as he stood up, and walked out the door.

Crawling to the window, she knelt beside it, and lay her palm against the cool glass. He looked up and did not wave. He looked away, drove off around the corner and out of sight.

She cried.

Two days of crying went by.

Calling him was never an option, in her mind. She knew that when someone decided on a course of action, no one could prevent it. She also realized that he had the courage to tell her, face to face. She had never experienced a man so direct, a man so honest. She could tell, that it was not easy for him, but it was harder on her.

Watching the bay for a couple of hours quietly, she did not see, the sailing boats, the sun and the cars on the street, go by. She sat quietly, sadly, wondering how she lost a man she barely knew and had fallen in love with, so quickly.

She met many men, yes, but she did not fall in love, so easily, neither did she get hurt, so fully.

But, where was this coming from, anyway. She never intended to meet anyone. How could she have fallen in love so easily, so quickly.

Was it possible, that she did not know herself as well as she thought she did? Was it possible, that all this blubber and bluster, about not meeting anyone, and 'simple conversation', was self protection?

Where was this protection now? What was she doing? Why was her heart breaking, so thoroughly?

Those were questions, Salma could not answer, because she had kept herself protected in that self preservation cocoon, of hardness and self reliance.

How could a woman at her age, with her experience, fall in love so quickly, allowing herself to be so heartbroken?

Questions about herself, kept swirling around. Focusing on them, was a disaster. Nothing good ever came of that nonsense, nothing.

Men had left her before. This was not a new concept; but none ever came to her door to tell her, face to face. It was usually, a disappearing act.

The ringing of the telephone, woke her of her reverie. She walked towards it, checking the caller ID. It was, Jamie. She pushed the accept button on her cell phone.

"Allo."

"Salma? Salma, is that you? It's Jamie."

"Yes, yes I know. How are you, Jamie? What's up?"

"Hey girlfriend, what is wrong? You sound, awful."

"I just got dumped by that guy, you know, the one you met only a week ago…"

"Hey, let me come over," she interrupted. "We'll talk. I will bring the wine. It'll cheer you up."

Jamie hung up and within an hour she was at Salma's with two bottles of Merlot, a bottle opener and two wine glasses. She stripped off the lead foil cover, piercing the cork with her bottle opener, she poured out the red liquid in a large glass.

It was like a dream, watching Jamie; open the bottle of wine. Zoning out, Salma watched, with glassy eyes.

Jamie poured the blood colored liquid in the big round shiny glass. When she started to pour another, Salma shook her head, covering the other glass.

"Not for me, Jamie. I do not drink, much wine."

With a toss of her head, Jamie sauntered, with her glass of wine and bottle, to the deck.

"What happened, sister?"

"You know, this guy I met on line, the one you met here, you know!"

Jamie nodded.

"Yeah, what's his name, ummm, Merrick?" answered Jamie.

Salma nodded.

"We hit it off. We talked, walked, slept together...," she trailed off, as tears streamed down her face.

Recounting the encounters of the last few days, Jamie listened, as Salma told the short story. When she was done, she sat back and looked at her friend.

"He will call," said Jamie, smiling, and waving her glass of wine. "You'll see, he'll call."

"He will not. I don't think so."

She looked around in a daze.

"I don't think he will call. What kills me is that I got so attached. How is that possible? How is it possible to get that attached in seven days, Jamie."

She wiped her face, angrily.

"How is that possible? What is wrong with me?"

"Nothing. It's normal. We all feel it when it happens. It has nothing to do with how long or how short the time, we know them. It hurts, dude!"

"Yes. It does. It does. Me, who always felt that I am free of this kind of thing, free to do, be, wherever and whenever."

Looking around her, she stopped, lost in thought.

"Salma, he'll call."

Looking over, Salma realized that Jamie was getting drunk. She was drinking alone, after all.

"Hey, how about spending the night here, Jamie?"

"Nah, I like to sleep in my own bed. It is Sunday too, and tomorrow, I have to be at work, early."

"You okay, to drive?"

"Yes, of course."

"Are you sure? You really could sleep here…."

"Nope. It's time to leave and go to bed, actually," interrupted Jamie, slurring.

Jamie stood up and seemed to lean over slightly. Salma reached over to steady, but never, touched her friend.

"I'm fine. I'm fine," she said, swaying slightly.

She walked towards the door. She had polished off two bottles of wine, all by herself.

Salma did not realize how late it was until she noticed the time on the microwave in the kitchen. The clock she set, since she did not need anyone else.

"Wow," said Jamie. "It's so late. Ten o'clock."

"Yeah," said Salma. "Time for bed."

"Good night, Salma. He'll call."

Leaning over, she kissed Salma, then walked down and out, to her car.

Salma slept fitfully that night. She did not do any better the night after either. Tuesday morning, she opened her e-mail and there was a letter from him.

She stared at the heading, without reading.

Salma stared.

She was not expecting this. She was not expecting anything, really.

She opened his e-mail.

Sonia Rumzi

WHY

You were born with wings. Why prefer to crawl through life?

          - Rumi

-Sell your cleverness and buy bewilderment.

          - Rumi

-Why do you stay in prison
when the door is so wide open?

          - Rumi

Subject: more of why   *Tue Sep 30 2003*
To: The Scribe   *From: Searcher*

Dearest Salma,

I feel there's a need to give you a much better idea, of why.

At this very moment, this morning, riding another fucking bus, there's an underlying anger ripping through my blood. How could I have allowed myself to become so easily entranced? It would be sooooo easy to simply tell myself, "It was the unforgettable experience of your tight warm body", or "God, the way you enjoyed devouring me". Salma, this physicality is only one aspect; you offered me everything I could wish for, giving me the opportunity to become -fully-lost within my own fragile mentality.

I needed (still do) to converse with a deep, thought

provoking realist, someone who sees the world for what it actually is - giving me a glimmer of how & where I might best point my skills & energies, to assist others.

It is for the sake of all others, I won't give into my narcissistic fantasies, my seemingly unending & unbridled lust. I know myself well enough, that doing so would become a disaster. It's easy for me to dive into that pool, never returning. In effect, drowning within my fractured anguish.

I need my partner to experience the world from a completely holistic & integral perspective. The raging river carves rock, and spills into placid pools; if we were to ever make it together, the gamut of humanism must be available to each of us.

Right now, today, I can't thank you enough for showing me just how unready I am for this relationship I so desperately need. Meeting you on the bridge opened my eyes, showing me the vast faults I still cling to.

My best guess as to the reason I can't accept your key today is compassion, for myself & others. In the next 20 - 30 years, life as we know it, won't be. I won't allow myself to become stagnant within my mental & physical pleasures. By accepting the submissive part of you, we would be doing just that.

In the next few months, I'll be working my ass off to be ready for the life I need. Where I work must change, yet I don't know what this means. Those I'm close to, must be a part of the flowing river within & around themselves too. However, finding others who are capable of such is no easy task.

Unfortunately, for a moment, I allowed myself to touch another deeply, hurting her. By accepting your key as presented, greater harm would've been done to both you &

myself, an unacceptable result.

Crazily, if you can understand what I've tried to convey within this, possibility remains open for us - but likely not at this time. There's too much to do, integrating the whole...

All my Love,
Merrick

Not sure whether she should answer or not, kept Salma, annoyed. Why should she bother? Why? Sitting back in her chair, she looked at the words.

Salma had never 'gone back', to anyone. Any man who broke up with her, ended up, out of her life, for good. So, why should she answer this? Why did she feel so compelled, to answer this e-mail. This man whom she did not know, that well. This man, who broke her heart, for no good reason.

Yet, what if this, was the man, for her? What if this was her mate for life? What then? Should she walk away from happiness?

Out of her element! Salma felt out of sorts. She was glad that he contacted her, yet apprehensive, at her decisions.

Everything she understood from his writing, so far, was that Merrick was confused, about what her expectations are, of him. Also, that he felt guilty, about his wife, Toni. He seemed taken aback, by this new passionate involvement, without ending his relationship with his x-wife.

Fear of the future, how quickly they felt for each other. All this, combined with his needs, physically and emotionally, created confusion; that led to fear and escape.

Sighing at her inconsistencies, she decided, to answer.

How to answer?

Deciding to take his e-mail, bit by bit, and answering succinctly, she sat in her chair, shaking her head.

This was a Salma, she did not recognize. A new Salma, not improved, just seeming desperate.

Subject: Re: more of why   *Tue Sep 30 2003*
To: Searcher   *From: The Scribe*

You have misunderstood! You never gave me a chance to show you. I would have accepted all of you. I loved your mouth on me. I was learning too. You took that away from me to learn to accept being loved and being done to and adored.

Together we would have loved others. Together we could conquer. I was still learning your body. I was still finding out about you. I was entranced by your beauty and your inner beauty.

Learning and growing does not come from running away! It comes from experiencing and teaching your partner. I could have learned so much from you. I could have learned to take as well as to give.

Instead, I will have to find someone who will use me instead of love me back, as you were doing. I learned so much from you in the one week we were together about accepting to be served as well.

I needed you as a lover and a friend, and you walked away fearing for your drowning. How sad!

You are afraid to be loved! You are afraid to be taken in

and warmed and cherished. I could have used the same form you and you would have taught me because of your gentleness and kindness and openness.

Offering you my apartment was as a haven. You could have used it to come and rest, contemplate, think, be! I guess offering too much is not something you are used to but no one I meet is ready for that.

You, and men like you, always do that. I have encountered this so many times. Fear of being loved and consumed by that love. It is a deep grounded love, Merrick. Not about Dominance and Submission, it is about giving yourself completely, learning to love completely. I am sorry you did not allow us that time.

I am well aware of my role in this world. I am a servant to people in general and that will never change. I have already told you that my commitment to God would never change because of you or anyone else but you did not believe me.

You are so used to making decisions for Toni that instead of allowing me to make my own decision, you decided for me that you are not what I need... How sad! I can make my own decisions, I am very capable and very strong. My love for you would enrich everything around me.

My love for you enriched my life and made me love more of those around me and embrace them.

The physical part was a learning, a savouring of beauty and devouring the physical need and the closeness it brought. No, it is not my tight ass or my mouth, it is the closeness it brought.

You were lost in the feeling that you got and the love that you felt from my actions and you freaked. You feel that you do not deserve that kind of love...I am sorry that you feel that way.

I wish you had given me the chance to love you!
I miss you very much.
Salma

Where was this overreaction coming from, anyway? Salma seemed so involved, she was begging. Since when, did she beg? She felt, as if, her whole life was warping around her. Could she stop this? Could she stop this carnage?

Why was it so important that this man be in her life? What was it about him, that made it so impossible, to move on at this time?

All this talk of being on her own, loving her life, loving her freedom and her independence, all, down the drain. All, in the span of one week.

Marveling at her own weakness, she continued to explain and cajole.

Subject: Re: more of why   Tue Sep 30 2003
To: The Scribe   From: Searcher

>…and you freaked.<
>you feel that you do not deserve that kind of love…<
Childhood pattern established, revealed again & again…
I'm having grave difficulties swallowing it's truth.
>I am pathetic…<

No my sweetness, your understanding is real.
More to follow as the tears subside.
-M

Subject: Re: more of why   *Tue Sep 30 2003*
To: The Scribe   *From: Searcher*

>you have allowed your imagination to run away with you.<

It's not imagination at all. Look at where I am today, right this moment, objectively, knowing I can lose myself in another.

Where does life go for us if this happens, and how could I possibly remain content?

We must be so *very* careful.

Your Love is boundless, but I require your absolute crystal clarity. Give it days & maybe weeks of exhaustive contemplation; fully realize what just happened, including the potential dangers & joys...

A conjoined, lifelong, *slowly* burning fire remains the vision, and I left her sitting beside it, alone.

I'm devastated, and afraid!

Yet, still writing...

-M

Subject: Re: more of why   *Tue Sep 30 2003*
To: Searcher   *From: The Scribe*

Love grows and pours over others because of the satisfaction that it creates within us. How wrong!

I am a realist. Always have been and I love people and have never allowed myself or my partner to forget that.

Getting lost in each other is a gift we offer each other. It does not close us to others. When we are filled with that love it overflows to others. Feeling pleasure and joy with someone does not eliminate our desire to please and serve others. Never!

Man and woman are completing each other. We found something that few people find and you are willing to throw it away based on guilt and myth! I wish you would not!

Salma

So, is that what this was? Is that true that she found what she was looking for, at last? And how come, she had no conscience idea, that she was on the prowl, searching, for the right man?

Every time, she read the e-mail, she copied then paste a sentence or a thought from it, then, explain the futility and the inaccuracies she saw in the logic.

She saw life differently.

Everything she explained, came from her own experiences of life.

Anger and annoyance at herself, and him, was bubbling, to the surface. He was making her, a needy person. Yet, she was a woman. She was in need. There was nothing wrong with being in need, of another.

She wanted to shake him, physically.

'Wake up! Wake up, you sleeping man.'

Subject: Re: more of why   *Tue Sep 30 2003*
To: Searcher   *From: The Scribe*

> I need life, so I won't seek a lifestyle.

You forget that I live life to the fullest-!! always! Come ride with me on life's adventure and see where it takes us, Merrick. I do not seek a lifestyle, I seek a partner who is open and reasonable and loving. I thought I found one! Don't deprive us of the joy of finding each other.

Salma

Subject: Re: Time!   *Tue Sep 30 2003*
To: The Scribe   *From: Searcher*

I need lunch and air...
With good fortune, some sun too...
-M

Subject: Re: more of why   *Tue Sep 30 2003*
To: Searcher   *From: The Scribe*

>Meeting you on the bridge opened my eyes, showing me the vast faults I still cling to<

Then allow me to go through this with you. Allow me to show you more. Allow me to love you and bring it out of you. Allow me to be loved by a wonderful man that I admire and care for. Allow me in! I need you too!

Salma

Subject: *Re: more of why*   Tue Sep 30 2003
To: Searcher   From: *The Scribe*

> By accepting your key as presented, greater harm would've been done to both you & myself, an unacceptable result.<

I am neither fragile nor stupid. My offer of the key was an open invitation for rest and love. You misunderstood. My need to serve is always there and my need to be served is also there.

You have allowed your imagination to run away with you. I am very practical and very grounded and I could have used your love in my life but you choose to take it away.

All for this idea that it would diminish something of our experiences instead of realizing that our love enhances all those other experiences and makes life bearable.

Knowing that you could come in my arms and talk to me and be loved and accepted as you are with whatever you are, is a gift from one lover to another. We found that! Don't take it away, Merrick. Let us learn, together.

Salma

Who did he think he was, telling her how to live, her life? Did he really think, that she was unaware of how, she should live, life?

Walking to the kitchen, she set the kettle on the stove, boiling some water, for tea. Then, turning on her CD player, she started some Baroque music. Bach drifted in the air, and calmed her senses.

As the water boiled, she turned off the stove, poured out water and picked up her tea, and went back to her desk.

Rereading the "why" e-mail, did not make things any better.

Does this mean, that she wanted, what she wanted; that she was irritated, because she was not getting it, now?

Finally getting angry, she wrote him. Feeling exasperated and frustrated, she wrote him.

Subject: Time!   *Tue Sep 30 2003*
To: Searcher   *From: The Scribe*

Merrick!

I am 47 years old …I am practical and down to earth! I found something I wanted and went after it…does that make me pathetically submissive or strong and knowing what I want??

I do not waste precious time. I just live life! I do not over analyze…I just live! I live life to the fullest and living and sharing with you makes me complete in so many ways.

If you let chances that are good and solid pass you by because you are afraid or because of old habits, you lose much.

It is not easy to open up my heart to people and get hurt but I choose to do that because it keeps me soft and pliable and approachable. I choose to love you…there is not "falling in love" about it. I choose to cater to you. I choose to adore you. I choose to still think that you may give us a chance, not because I am weak or stupid but because I know what I want.

Subject: Re: Time!   *Tue Sep 30 2003*
To: The Scribe   *From: Searcher*

>I do not waste precious time.<
Laughing my tired ass off, apparently I don't either!
>I choose to love you…<
It's an open moment of choice, which doesn't fade from the heart. Salma, my stupidity has no boundary. You've now seen it, clearly.
>I choose to still think that you may give us a chance<
As the artist touches the canvas, this possibility DOES exist. The underlying fear is: my all won't be enough; the depths of despair unrecoverable…
AND I have troubling difficulty allowing another to love me.
-M

Subject: Losing yourself!   *Tue Sep 30 2003*
To: Searcher   *From: The Scribe*

Merrick!
Losing yourself in another is not a crime! Losing our self in another is the ultimate way to become a butterfly to fly away and continue blessing others.
Keeping ourselves closed up tight and with walls around us to protect us from love is dangerous and will build calluses on your heart. Beware!
You are experiencing love! That is all! You are experiencing Agape Love. The giving, unexpecting, unconditional love

of a woman who adores you as you are, what you are and everything that comes with you and surrounds you.

That is why you are so afraid. You have never experienced it before. Allow me to show you, my love!

You are so precious to me, I would never allow you to get hurt or get yourself lost completely. I adore who you are, how can I let it get lost in anything. I like who you are, Merrick.

I like who you are. I like who you are!

I like your tears and your sadness and your joy. I like everything about you. I like your face and your hair and your joyous copulation. I like the surprise in your voice when you feel good. I like you.

I happen to like you. Just you, and what you are, and who you are.

Subject: Re: Time!   *Tue Sep 30 2003*
To: Searcher   *From: The Scribe*

> The underlying fear is: my all won't be enough, the depths of despair unrecoverable...<

Which one of us is capable of knowing what is enough, Merrick?? I give what I have, you give what you have. In time, we find out what is what! Take a leap of faith, you are an Aries! Unbounded bliss, remember?? Let your heart go, allow yourself to love and be loved.

We lose nothing but our inhibitions and our dogma. I would rather love for a season than never to love. I would rather be hurt than not ever to be allowed to love and be loved.

I do not shatter easily!!!! :-) I have not told you about my childhood. Maybe you will allow me to tell you face to face sometime. I have not told you of my marriage either, no time!

Can we try? Please, Merrick??
Salma

Subject: Life   *Wed Oct 01 2003*
To: The Scribe   *From: Searcher*

"Life shrinks or expands in proportion to your courage."
— Barbara Winter

Subject: Submit to Life   *Wed Oct 01 2003*
To: The Scribe   *From: Searcher*

Oh Goddess of Mine,
You are most wise.

I seek a spiritual partnership with you, side by side, walking along the path - together. Yesterday's email & last night's phone call laid down the first bricks in this foundation.

Here's one thing I can assure you. No matter what may happen in the future to my mental state, I'll make room for you to communicate with me. I completely underestimated you & your connection to God, and I'll endeavor to not let that happen again.

Your ability to LIVE amazes me.

Please show me how!

All my Love,
Merrick

Subject: Re: Submit to Life   *Wed Oct 01 2003*
To: Searcher   *From: The Scribe*

My sweet Man!

The day you took my hand on the bridge made me feel like coming home. You did not have to take it. We could have walked together separately but you did not. There is a longing and a yearning in you for connection and when you touched me, I knew!

God has never allowed me to walk with false feelings or false intuitions or false anything, He destroys anything false about me. He crushes and squeezes until I buckle.

More to come!

Salma

Subject: A story!   *Wed Oct 01 2003*
To: Searcher   *From: The Scribe*

The Vine-keeper took the ripe olives and put them in the crusher. The rollers went over the olives and they got mashed and ground under the pressure. The weight of the roller, the pain of the process did not mean much to the olive. The olive in that process was getting purified.

As the Vine-keeper looked on, the olive oil was pouring out of the other side into the large vat. He could smell the sweet smell of His olives. He watched the gentle pouring, slow and rhythmic.

As the end of the crushing came and the oil was dwindling down to drips and dribbles, He looked down into the clear liquid.

He smiled!

The Vine-keeper could see His reflection in the pure liquid.

When God allows us to be crushed by his hand or by the hands of others, it is to bring out of us the best of us. When He does what He does to purify and clarify, He can see His reflection in us and we grow in His love and knowledge of who He is and learn to be what He wants us to be.

With warm love and affection,

Salma

Subject: Re: A story!   *Wed Oct 01 2003*
To: The Scribe   *From: Searcher*

>The Vine-keeper could see His reflection in the pure liquid.<

LOL, just when I thought it safe to climb out of my cave, believing how you might be a realized dualist:

If you can see God in a bucket of crushed olive pulp, then my dear, you've got some non-dual oil in your reflection. :-)

>The day you took my hand on the bridge made me feel like coming home. You did not have to take it.<

Correct. This can only be experienced by two open hearts. If you hadn't been accepting of a hand, the kiss at the car wouldn't have happened. The day evolving into simple verbal communication, a parting of ways at the coffee shop - an opportunity lost.

However, you were open, and through it all, remain so. It's been amazing, to me.

Here's something you might find humorous. It's from my favorite astrologer; this from my ascendant, which is the astrological sign visible on the horizon at the exact moment of birth:

AQUARIUS (Jan. 20-Feb. 18): Are you afraid of what you want? Are you suspicious of success? Are you suffering from a hope deficit? Do you tend to go numb when in the presence of possibilities that should excite you? Then this week will be a boon. You will have the chance to pull off a rare form of exorcism — an exorcism not of grotesque demons and dumb-ass ghosts, but rather of the jaded cynicism that subtly corrodes your intelligence. Take this opportunity, my dear Aquarius, to cleanse yourself of the reflexive doubts that the world around you has brainwashed you into regarding as normal.

Oh, and just for good measure, our shared Solar radiations:

ARIES (March 21-April 19): Today and every day, five million lightning bolts will flash between earth and sky somewhere on our planet. At any given moment, two thousand thunderstorms are raging. While you may not be in the literal presence of one of these elemental outbreaks in the coming week, Aries, I believe you will channel a similar kind of energy: You'll be fiercely and tenderly alive with the blended force of primal fire and water. This doesn't necessarily mean you'll career out of control; you may be able to express the booming power in its most constructive form, cleansing and clarifying everything you touch.

Claude Flay's words often make me smile, especially when viewed the following week, after the facts are in.

Merrick

'Here he goes again,' thought Salma, bewildered. 'What in the world is he talking about?'

Realizing that Merrick did not talk that way when they were together, she felt confused, at these strange New Age references. They seemed to run on, forever. She skipped most of it.

Again her eyes fell on the text. He wrote about astrological signs. She smirked.

'Like a blonde teenager.'

Was this the man that she had been looking for all her life? This being who saw life through astrological charts and signs?

Flummoxed at the inconsistencies in herself, Salma sat back down, looking at the words on the screen. Life cannot be that cruel.

'Oh yes, it can,' her rational self, suggested.

So, when she found a gentle, loving man, he had to be nuts.

Subject: Re: A story!   *Wed Oct 01 2003*
To: Searcher   *From: The Scribe*

>you may be able to express the booming power in its most constructive form, cleansing and clarifying everything you touch<

I sure hope so! Nothing is worth trying that is easy. I cannot appreciate it as much…:-)

 Salma

Subject: take what you want   *Fri Oct 03 2003*
To: The Scribe   *From: Searcher*

She coyly asked: "Can we make love?"

One day she may be comfortable, no longer asking; choosing to let the river's current provide the flow. Until then, a more appropriate question might be, "How much time do we have…"

Merrick

Subject: Re: take what you want   *Fri Oct 03 2003*
To: Searcher   *From: The Scribe*

I am sorry that I delayed you yesterday. I could not help myself seeing you and holding you. I also needed you. I ask, so that I would not do anything you do not want. Give me that! I do not want you, uncomfortable. I always want you... so, you have to set the pace ...I would never tire of you in my mouth or inside me, no matter where we are and no matter what I am doing and no matter who is there...:-)
I did take what I wanted!
Salma

Subject: Re: take what you want   *Fri Oct 03 2003*
To: The Scribe   *From: Searcher*

LOL,
This is why I don't like email. You misunderstood. I wasn't "delayed", actively choosing to stay until just past sunset. What I meant is:
>I always want you... so, you have to set the pace ...<
Asking "Is it all right?" is silly. On the basis of desire, I'll not refuse you - anytime, almost anyplace. Just remember, try not to make others "too" uncomfortable, don't educate little ones, and keep from being arrested. Other than these kinds of considerations, opportunity is almost boundless.
If you hadn't leaped off the couch so quickly, there would have been a kneeling man between your legs!
>I would never tire of you in my mouth or inside me, no matter where we are and no matter what I am doing<
There are certain physical restraints, like when you're

133

driving!
>no matter who is there…:-)<
</grin>
You didn't seem to want me naked with your boss around!!!! Maybe it's best, because she might have been offended???
-M

Subject: Re: take what you want   *Fri Oct 03 2003*
To: Searcher   *From: The Scribe*

No, no! That is not what I meant, really! I did not misunderstand. I knew what you were saying. I meant that you wanted to stay of your free will. :-)
I want you to know that everything you do is alright with me, Merrick… whether you stay or go :-(….. I want you to feel that you can do whatever you want to do with me and around me.
I love you, Merrick. I want you to be happy no matter what the cost. I love you deeply and truly.
Salma

CLOWNING AROUND

Silence is the language of God, all else is poor translation."

- Rumi

Hanging up after a sweet conversation with Merrick, Salma smiled. Back on track! There was no ambiguity, about their relationship, now. They would be together until something different came up, or they tired of each other.

How much more complete could their lives be, now? Spending time together, precious time, until, she either stayed for good, or left, for another job assignment.

Having the day off, an idea rolled around in her head. He had to be at work, and she knew some of his routines, by now.

Arrive at work by eight, have lunch around one, outside, somewhere, in San Francisco. He liked the outdoors, and enjoyed spending time in the open air, eating and resting.

She went shopping.

Stopping, at World Deli on Lucky Drive, she bought a wicker basket, with a lid.

Then, stopping at Mollie's Market in Sausalito, she bought a small container of wild rice, another of fall squash, with cranberries and nuts, plus chicken skewers for good measure.

Hurrying over, to the fruit section, she bought a fresh mango, a box of strawberries, one of blueberries and another of raspberries.

Next stop, the pharmacy, in Marin City, for construction paper and a black felt pen.

Driving home, she thought of the timing of her plan. At home, preparing and cutting up the fruit, placing it in a flat container, the schemer, placed everything, in the basket with a fork, knife and spoon, adding lots of napkins.

With a felt pen, she wrote what she wanted to communicate on the construction paper. Placing everything in the basket, she put the notes on the very top.

Dressing in black from neck to toe, she hardly recognized herself. She covered her face in white, clown makeup. Yes, Salma did have clown makeup. Her alter ego, the clown. Made up her eyes, soft, with a black liner and a blood red mouth; topping it all off with a black beret.

Grinning, she got in her car. She wanted to see the expression on his face, when she showed up, all crazy and silly.

Stopping at the flower shop, she bought a single flower, on the Bridgeway shop, where the flower girl, smiled, commenting: "I really, like your job."

Salma did not correct her.

Driving across the Golden Gate Bridge, to the Financial District, where Merrick worked, in a publishing company, Salma enjoyed the scenery.

Parking her car was no easy task, but after she found a spot, she walked in the building, with her basket.

Arriving at the desk, she placed her basket down, opened it with exaggerated motions, pulling out her cards. She held the first one up, to the receptionist, who laughed.

"Good Afternoon," the card, said.

"Hello," said the stunned woman, behind the counter. "May I help you?"

"Merrick Wilson, please," said the next card.

The woman, seemed unaware of who Salma meant, then shaking herself, said, "Sure, you want me, to call Merrick, down?"

Salma nodded her head vigorously, in exaggerated mock approval.

A suited man, passed by, saw her holding the sign that mentioned Merrick, exclaiming, "Oh for God's sake!" storming off.

Salma thought how angry that man sounded. Poor thing! He needed a clown in his life. She smiled and waited.

Meanwhile, the receptionist spoke quietly into the mouth piece of the telephone.

The clown, saw the man she loved, coming down the stairs. He froze, when he saw her. She pulled out, the next card.

"Hello," she held, up.

"Hello," he said, smiling, then laughing as he came closer. Standing a few feet from her, his face was beaming with joy.

"Someone loves you very much," said, the next card.

He nodded.

With a flourish, she handed him, the flower. He took it and held it close to his heart.

She held out the next card, "This someone, thinks you are very special."

Grabbing the swaying helium filled floater, she handed him the balloon, with the smiley face on it.

"She wishes you a shining, sunny day," said, the next card.

He nodded, again.

This time, he had tears in his eyes.

"Would you like some lunch?" asked, the next card.

"Yes," he said, sounding choked.

Bending over at the waist while flapping her arms around, she picked up the basket, then handed it to him.

"Have a wonderful day," said, the next card.

Next card, "You are very loved."

Before he said anything, she turned on her heels and bounded out the door to her car and drove away.

Catching him by surprise, he had gone out to ask her to join him for lunch, and was disappointed that she disappeared.

Later, he told her, that, he was the talk of the office, for days.

E-MAIL BUDDY

Who could be so lucky? Who comes to a lake for water and sees the reflection of moon."

- Rumi

A note from one of the three men who answered her original Craigslist e-mail.

Subject: What a nice story!   *Thu Oct 02 2003*
To: Salma <The Scribe>   *From: PepeCheeseHead*

Ah, Salma…

You got snapped up! Desole! Who knows? Had I played it differently maybe you and I could be cooing with one another in French! Where did I go wrong?

DO NOT answer that question! Ce n'est pas important! Really! (I FORBID you to answer that question! My nervous system could not handle it!)

Because…from your story I have come to realize that I am in no condition to begin a relationship. Even with someone as charmante as you are.

Strange thing. I do not even "know" you and have never seen you (I did not cheat and go to Moonbeam between 6 and 7 to lurk and spy). Yet, without bandying about the cheapened word "friends", our e-friendship has been great fun and of great value to me.

I mean…I could actually VISUALIZE you (romantically)

meeting on the bridge! It was as if I were there! And it was as if I were projecting myself into his place and taking your hand! (I can do all of this because it is VERY obvious from your e-mail voice tone that you are smitten with this fellow. You "sound" soft and dreamy. The way I would like a woman to "sound" for me.)

But as "I" took "your" hand on the bridge in this visualization, I all of a sudden had this SERIOUSLY sinking feeling of the emotional responsibility required.

Humm.... had not thought of that before! How could I? I have no "thought" experience of the swoon quality of a woman who has just met a man she can like. Until you wrote me your last e-mail. How could I? Only a man's buddies and a woman's girlfriends get to "hear" this stuff.

I know (actually I don't know) that I am sounding seriously nuts here but I am thinking that you are understanding exactly what I am attempting to say.

Which is...

I am not thinking that I am wanting to put any woman in the "swoon state" if I am not prepared to take care of it. Meaning...perhaps it is time for me to cease being careless with my libido and take serious stock about the "effects" of it.

Yeah, I would like the warmth of a woman and, no, I am not interested in a LTR with anybody but myself right now. So what have I been doing?

Casting around on Craigslist to wow and zow an unseen woman with my graceful words and my charming humor? To what end? As an exercise in my "remote" abilities? (I am beginning to think so.)

So it is SO perfect that you wrote me that e-mail today! For I have been looking for a way to get out of my (developing) obsession with logging on to CL to see who I can charm for how long!

You have given me the key! Again, a window into the possible EFFECTS of my animistic keyboard antics.

No...don't want to do that any more! For, if I really love women as much as I say that I do, then I must be very careful with their hearts and not simply attempt to manipulate them so that I can once again experience the beast with two backs.

When one is younger, especially when a male is younger, he is much more careless about these things. (Why so many women are so deeply bruised?) (This is beginning to explain it!)

Well, then, your e-mail has cured me! No more Craig's List for me! No more keyboard pixie dust! (No more pixie dust at all!)

I am just going to chill for a while. Like in having instantly grown up!

Which does not mean that I will be impervious to some lovely who has her eyes wide open wishing to be on the receiving end of what I have to give.

(I may be crazy but I am not stupid!) But as of this moment I am no longer going to pretend to promise more than I wish, or am able, to give.

Does any of this make sense, Salma?

How liberating your e-mail has been for me?

I am one happy camper now! Amplified by how happy I am for you!

So will you continue to write to me off and on? To let me know how it is going?

I will still look for you at the Toronto but if you are with your fellow I will not make myself known.

(Are you watching the beautiful sunset tonight? The blue and pink, now blood red one as I (stop) typing this?)
HAPPY HAPPY! THANK YOU THANK YOU!
Francis (Francois)

So, this was why she wanted to make it work with Merrick. This was the reason for all the craziness and all the changes in her resolve. Finding the right person. Knowing the possibilities that could escape you and holding on, so that they would not.

It was getting clearer why she was working so hard at it, why her mind was changed, so quickly.

INSECURITIES

Knowest thou not the beauty of thine own face? Quit this temper that leads thee to war with thyself."
                                                                    -Rumi

Subject: Good Morning   *Mon Oct 06 2003*
To: Searcher   *From: The Scribe*

Hello Merrick!

I have not heard from you and of course miss you. Whatever it is you are thinking, share! Do not close doors. I love you!

I am not giving up on you that easily until you tell me to go away. So tell me to go away! Tell me you never want to see me again or hear from me again. Otherwise you will hear from me.

Did you go to the house to a disaster? Did you start feeling that you should not have been away for so long?? Did you feel that your life is better and that hers is not and that should not happen??

Don't shut me out! Remember what you told me? You promised to keep open communication. You know me now, Merrick. I will understand, whatever it is…just talk to me… please!

Subject: Re: Good Morning!   *Mon Oct 06 2003*
To: The Scribe   *From: Searcher*

>I have not heard from you and of course miss you. Whatever it is you are thinking, share! Do not close doors.<

The door is open, the fresh air flowing freely in.

I've been up to my eyeballs in stuff, especially this AM - Monday morning is diabolical. Having spent a glorious time with you, I returned to Toni's home to more of the same, with little in the way of real communication.

I'm not shutting you out, that's simply your insecurity speaking in your ears. What I am doing, is slaving away doing countless crapola this morning... I haven't had a moment to grab a glass of juice!

-M

Subject: Sigh of relief!　　　　　　　　　*Mon Oct 06 2003*
To: Searcher　　　　　　　　　　　　　　*From: The Scribe*

Thank you, Merrick! Yes, they are my insecurities. I will do better. Kisses!

Salma

Subject: Re: Sigh of relief!　　　　　　　*Mon Oct 06 2003*
To: The Scribe　　　　　　　　　　　　　*From: Searcher*

>I will do better.<

When I'm too damn busy to eat, there's not much room for much else. Right now, it's not a fun time in the park.

Before I go attack the next fire, I'm *getting* myself some apple juice...!

-M

Subject: Drive!   *Mon Oct 06 2003*
To: Searcher   *From: The Scribe*

I would like to pick up and drive you to work tomorrow. May I? Or do I do what you told me before, just take what you want. Therefore, I do not ask but show up and pick you up because I want to??

:-)

Salma

Sonia Rumzi

AM PICK-UP

Most people guard against going into the fire, and so end up in it.

> *- Rumi*

Let yourself be silently drawn by the stronger pull of what you really love.

> *- Rumi*

Sausalito always looked beautiful in the morning.

Waking up at five and stretching, feeling good and alive, Salma lay before her windows overlooking the bay. The view of the water, she saw, from her corner on the futon.

Her yoga mat was her friend and companion. As was routine for her morning, she stretched for 20 minutes, attempted to concentrate on the different asanas, breath, posture, yet thinking, of what the day ahead, held for her.

She was picking him up that morning from, Rohnert Park. It was better than a ride on the bus, that took him two hours. Spending that "dead" time with him, was definitely better. Two hours that she could spend with him.

Languidly, she got in the shower, washed lazily, feeling all the places he touched her, grinning, to herself. She smiled a lot lately, well, more than usual, anyway.

Drying herself off quickly, flipping her hair over, the daring woman, swung her head back and it lay where it needed to be in wet curls. Perhaps, one of her better features.

Her preferred cologne, Anais, went on next. Placing it

behind her ears, cleavage, behind her knees and on wrists, Salma thought of Anais, and her stories. This old biddy, was weaving her own tales, with this new love.

Reaching in her closet and pulling out what she was going to wear, Salma felt, alive.

Wrapping the black garter around her waist, and clipping it in place, then, stretching the matching bra over her breasts, she clasped it on.

Putting her long leg on the counter, she pulled up the silk stocking over muscular calves and up shapely thighs. She hooked the garter to the lace of the stocking, snapping it, in place, and repeated the same task, on the other leg.

Again her father, came to mind.

'You have long legs, like a camel,' he had, quipped.

Frowning at herself in the mirror, she moved away.

The sexy granny, came to the full length mirror and turned to look at her backside. Merrick liked that she had a small butt. She teased him that he must like men, because she had a boy's butt.

Slipping into her black raincoat, came next. Buttoning the lowest two buttons, she steadily, slipped on her four inch spiked black pumps, and headed out the door.

This granny thought she was well put together and ready for a rendezvous.

Salma's father used to say that, if a woman could not walk in high heeled shoes, she should not wear them. This was never an issue until, Salma, found herself faced with the aches and pains of, aging.

Her father, again. Maybe that was an issue that she should explore further. Not now. Later.

The air was crisp and the sky was bursting with color, perhaps, a reflection of the emotions, rolling through her.

Blues, deep reds, orange yellow and pink clouds, streaked the sky. In her car, Mozart's 24th, played. The adrenalin was pumping and her 40 year old body felt like it was back in its 20-s. She felt her nakedness and freedom as she drove North on 101 towards Rohnert Park.

40 minutes later, arriving, she veered to the right and went into the plaza to Moonbeam to pick up her coffee. Medium, four Splenda, bone-dry, cappuccino. Not an easy chore, for the best of the baristas. Once in a while, someone would take the time, making her a true cup of foam. Rarely, as it would appear today! She also ordered, a mocha for Merrick. How odd, that after only a short while, she could tell what his drink would be.

Taking the soggy cup of coffee and leaving to her car, the feelings of elation, had not departed from her. She arrived at the parking lot in plenty of time, always, painfully early.

She got out of the car, unbuttoning the only two buttons, as his little car turned into the parking lot. After he parked, he got out then walked toward her, with a smile.

Unaware of the surprise, he put his arms inside her coat.... and lo and behold, nakedness. He stepped back and the look on his face was unparalleled. He ogled her.

Taking a step back, while opening her coat, she twirled around, posing her legs forward, left then right, being frivolous and funny.

Desire, fueled him. Pulling her closer, with his hand on her bare back, he felt inside her coat.

"Easy access," she whispered, in his ear.

Running his hands over her silk stockings, pulling that leg up, she wrapped one stockinged leg around his pant clad thigh and he groaned in her chest. He was hard. 'No atrophy,' smiling to herself, 'ha'.

"We will get arrested," he said, "if we don't get out of here."

Getting in, on the passenger side, the intrepid woman, put her head, on his lap. He pushed her away.

"We will get arrested," he said, seriously. "It is against the law...."

Turning her mouth against him, made him choke on his words. Feebly, a few more times, he tried, to push her away. This did not deter her. So defeated, he allowed it. She looked up and he was smiling.

"You are smiling like a Cheshire cat, you nasty wench."

Laughing heartily, as she watched him fumbling with his zipper and adjusting himself, trying to concentrate on driving, she turned in her seat, sitting up, politely, like an angel.

"Now I know why this is so illegal. I couldn't reasonably, concentrate on driving, while this was going on," he smiled, tersely, still enjoying himself. "I can't believe that you had your mouth on me for the last forty five minutes."

Smiling, rather pleased with herself, she sat back for the ride. It seemed to be a successful morning, for both of them. It achieved what she wanted, got to spend time with him. And he, did not have to be on the long bus ride.

"Did ya have to wait long for me? I didn't think I was late."

"You were not. I am uncomfortably early, everywhere. But I would rather be waiting for you here than be anywhere else," she added. "So, no, you were not late."

They drove across the Golden Gate Bridge reveling in the glorious morning, with the sun over the city horizon, as they basked in each others' company.

"Isn't this better than the bus??"

"Infinitely!" he said, and reached again for her thigh.

Sighing her delight, she realized that he always kept his hand on her, somewhere, while they were together, and she touched him, lightly.

Sipping his mocha, he stole glances at her, while watching the road.

"This has lots of coffee, huh?"

"I think it has two shots," she said.

"Wow. I don't drink much coffee. Hopefully, I won't have a raging headache." He smiled, reassuringly, at her. "But, it'll be worth it."

Arriving at the Financial District, he got out of the car and she came around to the driver's seat and settled in. He leaned into the car and kissed her, sliding his hand under her coat and touching her bare skin, caressing her thighs and feeling her silks.

Kissing him back, and reaching for him, he quickly, swung away.

"No way," he said, laughing. "First, you come, like my teenage dreams, to pick me up. Now, you want me to walk into work looking like I have no self control, whatsoever??"

When he pushed her hand away with determination, she pouted.

"You can pout," he said, chortling.

"Should I pick you up this evening?" she asked, saucily.

"If you get done early enough, sure."

"I'll bring you back to your car."

He cocked his head. "Yes, you will."

Kissing her again, deeply, he went quickly around the back of the car and into the building where he worked.

Driving back to Marin, to work, Salma felt sexy, elated and content.

Subject: for today   Mon Oct 06 2003
To: The Scribe   *From: Searcher*

Two thoughts for you on this Monday:
The first was revisited upon seeing it hanging as a garden
signboard:

> "The earth delights to feel your bare feet
> and the winds long to play with your hair."
> "The Prophet" — Kahlil Gibran

The second thought drives me forward today, for it is the
peacefulness of your experience I long for, not the chaotic "is
everything all right result from the seeming distance."

Thus it is said; "If you want to know what you were doing
in the past, look at your body now; if you want to know what
will happen to you in the future, look at what your mind is
doing now."
from "Kindness, Clarity, and Insight"
— H.H., the 14th Dalai Lama Tenzin Gyatso

Yes, please pick me up - however, I'm not at all clear what
time this will be yet. Monday is usually quite challenging,
and I end up staying after 5:00 PM… I'll let you know about
the timing as things move forward…
With Love,
-M

PROFOUND EFFECT

One day You will take my heart completely and make it more fiery than a dragon. Your eyelashes will write on my heart the poem that could never come from the pen of a poet."

- Rumi

God turns you from one feeling to another and teaches by means of opposites, so that you will have two wings to fly, not one.

- Rumi

Subject: Point in Hand   *Wed Oct 08 2003*
To: The Scribe   *From: Searcher*

Dearest Salma,

You've had a profound effect on me, physically, emotionally, and to some unfolding degrees, spiritually too. Clarity is your luminescence, brought to light by Love.

Take a moment & imagine the experience. I can count on one hand the number of times desires of flesh have been indulged in at work. Ever since I can remember, I've always had a fertile imagination. Actually acting on such while at work has been an exceedingly rare event. When you mentioned being done yesterday, I needed you so desperately. I was overpowered by it, consumed, using my rough hands where I wanted the warmth of your soft moist lips. When it was over, tears remained. The desire satiated, the flesh yielding; a strong sense of loss, a reflected moment of striking exposure. How could this have happened? Is my life such an unbelievable mess? Why do I *need* a specific film scanner? Why is…?

Here, this may explain more. Each dances at the edges, missing the fullness of the specialness. From this week's scope:

AQUARIUS (Jan. 20-Feb. 18): "No work is more worthwhile than to be a sign of divine joy and a fountain of divine love." So says mystic and scholar AnSalma Harvey, and I fervently agree. Not everyone is cut out for such an exacting career, of course. The pay isn't great, the hours are long, and the heroes who make it their main gig rarely get the appreciation they deserve. It's best to try it out for a while on the side without quitting your day job. Having provided those caveats, Aquarius, I'm pleased to inform you that this is the best time in years for you to work hard at being a sign of divine joy and a fountain of divine love.

ARIES (March 21-April 19): "I've been practicing radical authenticity lately," my Aries friend Steve told me. "I'm revealing the blunt truth about unmentionable subjects to everyone I know. It's been pretty hellish — no one likes having the social masks stripped away — but it's been ultimately rewarding." I thought a minute, then said, "I admire your boldness in naming the currents flowing beneath the surface, but I'm curious as to why you imply they're all negative. To practice radical authenticity, shouldn't you also express the raw truth about what's right, good, and beautiful? Shouldn't you unleash the praise and gratitude that normally go unspoken?" Steve sneered. He thought my version of radical authenticity was wimpy. I hope you don't, Aries. you have an astrological mandate to be honest in both ways.

Salma, to be perfectly honest - you scare the piss out of me - delightfully! What's right, good, and overpoweringly beautiful is within sight along my path. Running is the easy & safe choice; doing so again, stupid, foolish. At no point in memory has this feeling of - Run & Stay - been so exacting. You've expanded me, in more ways than you know. Absolutely I'm "bigger", atrophy removed by active participation with who you are. My daily needs changed into profound moments, by your desire to taste a few drops from this body. You've been actively encouraging me to do what I don't know how to do. Of the women I've allowed in, none of them have pulled me in so many directions at once. You've given me the ability see how small I've been, and how much more I might be.

To be sure, I'm not at all certain I can live in a Texas cave, and I'll show you why one of these weekends. I'm in no rush, the weather has continued to be "too nice" right now, lacking any real intensity. As Winter approaches, I'll share much more of this with you. At the same time, it doesn't matter - living is the need, the where & how of much less importance.

You seemed surprised at the amount of "stuff" I did yesterday afternoon/evening. It's vital for me to get rid of more each day than comes in. The problem only grows worse if I don't continue on such a path of diligence. The portable I've been working on has been as a favor to one of the employees I work with. I could've turned it over to my assistant Rose, but this one I wanted to do myself. Validating what I know how to do, a grounded feeling of ability. In the end, meaningless.

>It always happens when I do things without spiritual direction.<

My personal spiritual direction can become deluded by

desire, perceived needs. This is why you scare the piss out of me. Will my desire to Love, Fuck, and Be with you consume the spiritual connection I seek with you? Will we allow our little selves to be enslaved by ourselves?

There's so much to say, so little needing said.

God I need, want, and adore, you & you!

Merrick

Salma marveled at the length of the e-mail. But when she read it, she thought suddenly that this man was a 'whack job'. She covered her mouth with her hand, at the thought.

Who was this man who wrote this… this weird stuff? Who writes like this? What was this that he wrote, anyway?

It was like falling into the mind of the Charlie Manson of peace and love.

Sighing, she read again.

A New Age man or a very confused and anxiety ridden, man. Who knew!

Salma decided to answer only the parts that made sense to her in that strange e-mail. An e-mail that seemed to come from a strange mind. Should she pursue this?

How stable was this man who could write such drivel? Was it drivel? Or was he so confused, that he wrote out of an imagination, wrought with delusion.

Again, she decided to answer the parts that, made sense to her. The rest, she would discard, as the rantings of a very nervous human being.

Subject: Re: Point in Hand   *Wed, 08 Oct 2003*
To: Searcher   *From: The Scribe*

> Will my desire to Love, Fuck, and Be with you consume the spiritual connection I seek with you? Will we allow our little selves to be enslaved by ourselves?<

I could not allow nor would allow myself to be in that state my darling...I have lived my life for God. I work for him, I live for him, I do for him what I believe he wants me to do. I cannot allow you or anyone else to consume me to the point of not growing spiritually.

What I am trying to tell you is that together, walking a loving, open, peaceable path would lead to open sharing of all those things that we both need and that God has in store for us.

I am not sure why I scare you. I do not understand it that well, since I do not think so much of myself in the spiritual realm. I only seek to love the way God has taught me to love. Love is patient and kind, it is not boastful, it does not see offense. I have learned to love through the Master of Love.

But, I have to share with you, one of my past lovers laughed when I mentioned to him that you could not see me again. He told me that he understands completely. He wants a crack at it again...:-) but I could not. So, I guess there is someone out there who understands what you are talking about.

I am just me...never have been more or less. God help me, I can be such a bitch and so unkind that I wonder why God ever puts up with me. But it passes and He forgives me and I move on.

Please please don't run! I could not stand it! I love you so much!

Salma

Subject: Re: Point in Hand   *Wed Oct 08 2003*
To: The Scribe   *From: Searcher*

>Please please don't run!<

Don't misunderstand. It's not that I'm about to do so - what I'm trying to convey is the equal stretching of Merrick with the opposing forces of Run & Stay.

5:00 PM or so out front?

-M

Subject: Re: Point in Hand   *Wed Oct 08 2003*
To: Searcher   *From: The Scribe*

Yes, yes... I understood :-) !! I just need to say it... for me and for you to hear it.

Loving someone is time. Time is the only true test of love, of authenticity. One can say the words and claim much with the lips but time proves us in the end.

I have lived so far with an open heart... I would rather have my heart ripped out daily and stomped on, than close it up and protect it. My faith has taught me that, just so I could remain soft and malleable in the hands of the Potter.

Knowing that, I cannot allow you or anyone else to get in the way of my true happiness which is my relationship with God. Before I met you on the bridge, I prayed. I knew I should meet you and so I went. When you left me that Sunday, I did not hold you, I knew that I had to let you go... so I did. Direction has been my mainstay Merrick, love has been the core in all my dealings.

I remember telling you that I have things but don't own them and you laughed. It is true! Some day you will understand where I am coming from with that. I have need to use things but if they are gone, I can do without. I have come without anything and plan on leaving with nothing… no choice there really.

My whole experience living here in the States has been one great big adventure and blessing. Sometime we can talk more about it. I am grateful and appreciative all the days of my life and hope that this feeling will never change. It keeps me humble and clear headed.

My job comes from blessing; my daughters are a gift for a time that I had to mould and teach to become Women of God, functioning adults, loving beings.

You have been my newest blessing and I adore you. I adore every part and piece of you. I adore your mind, your body, your very soul. I could not allow you to get lost. What we share is very physical because we are starving for affection and touching. We are learning, like a child given a new toy, learning what makes it "tick". Be patient!

You have loved me in this short while more than any man has in many many years. Thank you! Allowing me to taste you, to be with you, to share with you, to love you has been a joy and a blessing…. I pray it keeps growing in my heart. I wish I could have more of you. I have not shown you how I can love yet.

Salma

Subject: Holding!   *Thu Oct 09 2003*
To: Searcher   *From: The Scribe*

My sweet man,

Holding you last evening was probably one of the most wonderful experiences I have felt in the last few months. It was good and quiet. It was affectionate and near.

Yes, I could feel that you would have drifted off to sleep if you could have and it hurt immensely that you could not and so you slept on the couch.

I want to hold you longer and closer and deeper whispering loving sweet somethings in your ear and kissing it.

I love you Merrick.

Salma

Subject: Sounds!   *Thu Oct 09 2003*
To: Searcher   *From: The Scribe*

My name coming from your mouth in pleasure amazes me all the time. I hear it many times in my head when I am alone. There is a tenderness and love in it that I have not ever heard before.

Your sweet soul pours out over me and surrounds me and keeps me warm. I know that you think you do not do much to reciprocate (in your mind) but allowing me in is a huge deal to me. It keeps me focused and wanting.

Love is not an idea…it is action and a living power. It cannot be hoarded or collected, it cannot be bought or sold but it is a gift to be given. Now, when it is received, it is even more powerful. The act of loving expands the heart and soul for the giver and the receiver. The giver is blessed and the receiver is humbled and the reverse is true, the giver is humbled and the receiver is blessed.

Thank you for allowing us this experience. Thank you for allowing me to grow in the warmth of your love and tenderness. I can see it expanding and spilling over to the people around us because if we know that we are loved, we

can share the pleasure and the joy of our happiness.
Your loving partner,
Salma

Subject: Re: Sounds!   *Thu Oct 09 2003*
To: The Scribe   *From: Searcher*

>Thank you for allowing us this experience.
Your loving partner<

Ohhhhh…..
Tears nourish where a glass of juice cannot. Thank you
for beginning my day with such delight.
As in most things, the world around me reflects what's
happening inside. As I gazed into the vast Pacific today, the
waves were much larger than normal for Fall…
With sweet tears,
Merrick

Subject: Love's Touch   *Thu Oct 09 2003*
To: The Scribe   *From: Searcher*

If the body feels tired for even a moment, have it remember
where my lips have been!   :-))
Merrick

Subject: Re: Love's Touch   *Thu Oct 09 2003*
To: Searcher   *From: The Scribe*

Thank you my darling…I miss you!
Salma

Subject: This morning's meditation!   *Fri Oct 10 2003*
To: Searcher   *From: The Scribe*

For the greater my wisdom, the greater my grief. To increase knowledge only increases sorrow.

To enjoy your work and accept your life, that is indeed a true gift from God.

People who do this rarely look with sorrow on the past, for God has given them reasons for joy.

With all my love that comes deep in my soul,

Your,

Salma

Subject: Re: This morning's meditation!   *Fri Oct 10 2003*
To: The Scribe   *From: Searcher*

>For the greater my wisdom, the greater my grief. To increase knowledge only increases sorrow.<

Indeed, ignorance is bliss. Once removed, suffering becomes visible.

I'm finally moving, albeit, slowly, without ease.

I slept poorly last night, waking often. I've had a headache all morning, my stomach's been doing flips, and my appetite is way below normal. Energetically, I'm feeling drained.

Rest is needed, yet that's not a viable option just yet. Today's network switch is an important task. A short nap before going into the office may be helpful, and then again…

Thank you for sharing your meditative moment with me. Experiencing the deepest parts of you is a rare gift…

-M

Subject: Re: This morning's meditation!   *Fri Oct 10 2003*
To: Searcher   *From: The Scribe*

We will rest together. Holding you in my arms will be rest for me and hopefully for you as well. If I can convey to you my love by touch and feel then I have done what I want to do.

Mother Theresa said not to be concerned with doing "big things" but doing little things with "big love".

See you later,
Salma

TOO MUCH

Last night the moon came dropping its clothes in the street. I took it as a sign to start singing, falling up into the bowl of sky.

- Rumi

The moon has become a dancer
at this festival of love.
This dance of light,
This sacred blessing,
This divine love,
beckons us
to a world beyond
only lovers can see
with their eyes of fiery passion.

- Rumi

Merrick promised to pick her up that morning. He told her that he had a surprise for her, and to be comfortably dressed in slacks. He also mentioned going to dinner later that evening, and, "By the way, bring a bathing suit".

A stretchy pair of black lycra mix, pants with, a light, airy black top was her choice for the day, and hiking boots. Pulling open a small backpack, she put in, a brush, a towel, her bathing suit, a dressy scarf and sandals. Things that, she thought, she might need, for that day.

He came upstairs and they lay on the floor, cuddling and kissing. He stood, suddenly, pulled her up with him, smacking her behind.

"We'd better go, before we just stay indoors. It is a beautiful day."

They walked downstairs to the car; where he slipped into the driver's seat, then drove, off.

Heading east, towards Vallejo, nothing looked familiar to her, until, she saw the tops of the roller coaster tracks. She started to point, excitedly.

"O my God! I love roller coasters. Do you ride roller coasters?? I love to be on high and the excitement of the ride and the climb and then the rush coming down," she babbled.

"Yes, you told me," he said.

"Where are we going? Are we going anywhere near there?" she prattled.

"To the roller coasters."

Disbelievingly, she looked at him. Suddenly silent, she sat, quietly.

"You are serious?" she queried.

"Yes, I am. When we passed through here, you told me that you liked roller coasters. So, here we are. We are going to the roller coasters."

Too overwhelmed to say anything, she sat back and watched the coasters, coming closer. The brilliant colors of the tracks stood out, against the blue sky. Anticipating the excitement, the wonder of that excitement with Merrick, made her sit on the edge of her seat. Sharing something so trivial in her life, with someone she loved so much, was wondrous.

"Have you been on roller coasters?" she asked, tentatively.

"Not lately. I worry about the Gs and I have to be

careful."

"Gs?"

"Gravity. Gravitational units. My back can only handle about three, beyond that I am in trouble. Negative Gs, are a good thing."

"I still don't understand," she replied, amused.

"Positive Gs are when a coaster comes to the bottom of the hill and has to go up, rises, you know. Negative Gs when it is on top of the hump, and then coming down."

"Neither one bothers me," she said, childishly. "They just excite me."

He smiled as though to a penchant child. He patted her leg and she tittered.

Her whole day was laughing and smiling.

They buy season tickets to Six Flags Marine World, Africa USA. Season tickets meant more times to come, more time spent together, it meant he wanted to see her again, more than once even. Season tickets are for people who are, together.

They spent the day standing in line, longer than they rode any of the coasters. Even the standing in line was fun, was something to do, together. Standing in line meant chatting and just, being.

If someone had asked if this old woman was happy, she would have been able to respond, immediately, with a, yes.

Salma was so excited standing in line, waiting for her turn with Merrick. Dragging him to the front of the line, where the waiting was even longer, for the front seat, he looked at her, doubtfully.

"The front?" he asked, nervously.

"There is no reason to ride a coaster, unless you sit in the front, to see that ground, coming up, at you."

Grabbing his hand, she kissed it, in her excitement. He

patted her cheek.

"So, you are doing this for me only, huh?" she asked, in mock sarcasm.

"Just so," he answered.

"You will love it. The whole thing is just….." She took his hand, excitedly, kissing it again.

When their turn came, they sat in the front seat, nothing before them, nothing at all, well, except for the tracks.

Eyes widening, he looked at her.

"I am really, doing this," he said, sounding genuinely nervous.

"Yes, you are," she encouraged, touching his hand, which gripped the side bars.

Strapping themselves in while hanging onto the frame of the seat, the call came, and they were, off.

The floor fell away, and the weathered riders, felt elated.

The carriage started forward, up a steep hill clicking and clacking all the way. When it got to the top, there was not enough time to see the beauty of the vista, because within seconds, they were hurtling down the tracks, their eyes glued to the ground, coming up at them, so fast. Everyone was screaming in excitement, and exhilaration.

The roller coaster took several turns and dips, it flipped and turned. There was laughter and tense anticipation. Suddenly, it turned right, flipping three times, it turned left, flipping two more times, the other way.

It went up, around and upside down and back, jarred into place, on the tracks.

Suddenly, it came to a stop. A roar of disappointment arose from the riders.

Salma reached to touch Merrick's hand. He was lost, in joy.

As they got off the ride, he hugged her to him, tightly.

"You crazy, crazy woman. I have not done this in so many years. I like it."

He hugged her again, pulling out, the park map.

The next roller coaster was a ten minute walk. Hand in hand, the new couple, walked there. Standing in line chatting, kissing, talking, then riding, repeatedly, they seemed, in their own world.

The day was spent walking, observing and riding.

Feeding the giraffes was a joy. They enjoyed the lorikeets' antics and friendliness. As long as you had a cup of sweet drink, they alighted, on your hand or shoulder to get some. One courageous bird sat on Salma's head, climbed down her shoulder, down her arm, to the much coveted, nectar.

Salma was a child again, a happy child. She laughed out loud and pointed at the birds. Merrick, smiled at her love of life.

The tropical garden held beautiful butterflies of all shapes, sizes and colors. The keeper, told them to keep an eye out for the sloth. She lived in the trees. Finally, they saw her hanging on a branch. Salma had never seen a sloth.

High wires, held orangutans. Their blazing, orange red color made them look like, they were on fire.

Sitting on the stadium seats, watching the dolphins' antics with their trainers while wowing the crowd, Salma sat beside, Merrick content with life.

When he pulled out his phone, she knew time was running out. Looking around her, the woman, enjoyed the blue sky and the colorful surroundings, unaware of time. Nothing seemed to matter, while she was with, Merrick.

He took her hand and pulled her close to him.

"You look like you are having fun," he said, holding her

tightly, against his body.

"I am," she smiled, into his blue eyes. "Very much, indeed."

"We have to go," he said, kissing her mouth, before she had a chance, to protest. "They close at five anyway, and we have things to do and places to see."

As he always did, he took her hand, walking quickly and briskly, from the park, out to the parking lot, and into the car.

Chatting away while Merrick drove, Salma was trying to get information out of him, about, what they were to do, next.

He was reticent and secretive.

"Patience is a virtue," he said, wryly.

"One less virtue," she retorted.

Realizing that they were in Napa, as she read the signs all over the place, Salma only then knew, the general destination. Driving to Napa, the weather was getting warmer, as they came closer to the vineyards, smelling the wonderful aroma of crushed grapes.

Inhaling the new smells around her, she remembered that she still had boots on.

Reaching over, behind her, Salma got her bag. Then, pulling out her sandals, she put them on, after removing her boots.

Pulling her scarf out of the bag, wrapping it around her neck, voila; she was dressed for dinner.

Being a traveller, she was used to transforming her clothes from one use to another, and this, was just another one of those times.

He looked over and smiled.

"Just like that. No fuss, no muss. You've obviously, done

this before. No need for a bathroom or changing room or anything. Two seconds, and you are ready."

"Usually," she demurred.

He reached over, putting his hand on her thigh. Shivering, she held his. They were both warm.

"Here we are."

The parking lot of the vineyard where they turned in, to park, had a large sign that read, "Slix". Taking her hand, they walked, into the coolness of the restaurant.

"Can we get a table out back, please?" asked Merrick, of the young woman.

"Of course," she said, picking up two menus.

They followed her, through the chic restaurant, out the back doors to the patio, overlooking the vineyards, gardens and hills, in the horizon.

It was a spectacular evening. The sun was shining, and the glow from its rays, lit everything like fire, with light and shadow.

When they were seated, the hostess offered them the menus.

"Trevor, will be with you in a moment," she announced. "He will be your server, this evening."

After the young woman left, Salma, turned to Merrick.

"Wow, this is so beautiful. It is breathtaking."

"Yes, I thought you'd like this."

"Thank you," she said.

"Patience is a virtue," he replied, kissing her hand.

The waiter arrived to take their order.

"Good evening. My name is Trevor. I am your server for this evening. Can I get you something to drink?"

Salma looked over at Merrick.

"I am ready to order too, are you?"

"I'm ready," he said, surprised.

"Wonderful," said Trevor, the waiter, server.

"I would like some bubbly water and a glass with no ice." She waited, until he finished writing. "The steak, very, very well done, please, and a salad with vinaigrette dressing. Thanks," she said, handing the waiter her menu.

"Lemonade, no ice, please," said Merrick. "Chicken salad."

Trevor took away their wine goblets, as the bus boy came over, to fill their water glasses

The server walked away, to put in their order.

Stunned into silence by the quiet and the beauty around them, they watched the sun, disappearing behind the hills.

When the drinks arrived, they sipped the cooling liquid.

There seemed to be no tomorrow, or later.

Basking in the present moment, enjoying everything from the scenery to the fragrances of the evening, to most importantly, the presence of Merrick beside her, Salma looked at her surroundings.

'Like a movie or a novel,' she thought, to herself.

Merrick was somber, watching the horizon.

"Is everything alright?" she inquired.

"Every-thing's fine," he said.

Taking her hand, he kept it in his.

"Every-thing's just fine."

There was an intensity about him that she could not comprehend, yet. He seemed to feel so much. Looking over at the man beside her, she contemplated talking to him about that strange e-mail, but decided against it.

Their dinner arrived.

As usual, the steak was placed before Merrick; the chicken salad, though, was placed before Salma. Somehow, it was not possible in California, for a woman, to order the beef, while the man, ordered the chicken.

"May I get you anything, else?" asked Trevor, politely.

Both declined, needing nothing, at that moment.

When their waiter left, they exchanged plates.

"Happens all the time," she said, sarcastically.

They ate, silently. They ate quickly. There was no rush, but they seemed to be on work momentum, and they ate swiftly. It was not hunger, but time management.

When they were done, Merrick paid the bill. Taking her hand, he walked her down the garden path, no pun intended. The owners had built vegetable boxes and the kitchen staff used the produce, fresh vegetables and spices, that came out of it.

The garden was at the end of the season and the few peppers and tomatoes were hanging, on limp vines. The colors, were still amazing and bright.

Looking up at the horizon, they noted that the sun had set behind the hills, in the distance, leaving marvelous, exquisite touches, across the sky, and over the vines and leaves.

The vines, lay low, with the weight of the grapes, needing to be picked. Merrick explained, that some owners, chose to make their wines sweeter, by leaving the grapes on the vines, to ripen, to a higher degree, of sweetness.

Listening to him, as he whispered, when he talked, she leaned, closer. There was a hush, almost a reverence, to the scenery; and the quiet gave her peace of mind.

Half an hour after walking along the paths in the vineyard, enjoying the colors and the warmth, he slowly turned her around, heading towards the car.

Opening the car door for her, he waited until she sat in her seat. She watched him walk around to the driver's side.

Heading deeper into the Napa valley, she could tell, that they were not heading home, anytime soon.

Realizing, that she was totally dependent on Merrick, his sense of direction and decision making, she sat back in her seat, not recognizing anything, around her, just release.

Amazed at this time, they were having together, she closed her eyes.

Suddenly, making decisions was not her job. Suddenly, relaxing and letting someone else at the helm was alright. Always being in charge, was exhausting.

Nothing should matter but the present. Opening her eyes suddenly, she refused to close them again, lest she missed anything, around her. Looking over at Merrick, she watched him, intently, driving and focusing.

He noticed, reached over, and touched her leg.

If this day, ended it all, she would be sad. But, those hours would remain etched in her brain, as the way, good relationships, should be. This was the way people should make each other feel. She was content to die, realizing that she loved, and has been loved back.

Was that some sort of cliche in her head? This, same Salma, was the one who did not need anyone. The very same one, who did not want a relationship.

Who was this new Salma? Did she even want her around? This Salma, was a happy, content woman. This Salma, was not as sure of herself, as the arrogant Salma, who needed no one.

But the other, old Salma, was like an old coat or sweater, that fit perfectly and comfortably. This new, giddy vixen was unnerving, but exciting.

In a relationship, one should feel safe, comfortable, wanted and needed.

Merrick enjoyed being with her. This, in itself, was a huge achievement, in relationship terms. Not just doing things together, but liking her company. Not rushing the time with her, to do anything else, without her. He was not spending fast time with her, to do the next thing on his own. He was deliberate and slow, taking his time.

Merrick deliberately spent time with her. His mind did not seem to be focused on the next thing he would be doing, without her.

Much to get used to.

"What are you thinking?" he asked, suddenly. "You're frowning."

"Am I?" she rubbed, at her creased forehead.

She nodded.

"I am. I was thinking how wonderful my day has been. I am just thinking that if it all stops here, I would hold the memory, for the rest of my life."

"It won't," he said. "I want to live my life with you. To learn how to live my life, the way you do. You promised."

They drove in silence. A silence born of content and calm. An unhurried silence, based on trust and a time to come.

Feeling slightly car sick, as he drove the winding road, Salma realized, that she had never gotten sick before, because she was always, the driver, the designated driver.

Arriving at the City of Calistoga, the sickly grandma was turning green. Looking around her, noting the old buildings and the quaint street, she adjusted in her seat. Driving them down the main street, turning right then left quickly, to a back street, they came upon a beautiful white building.

Stumbling, she thankfully, got out of the car, after he parked, across the street.

Calistoga Spa was written in big white, scrolly letters.

Walking hand in hand towards the entrance, he got to the desk, asking for two passes for the evening, to the waters.

"It is still early," said the girl, with a nasally whine, from behind the desk. "You still have an hour, before you can go in."

"Yes," he said, patiently. "We will go have some coffee and come back by seven."

Taking her hand, and walking out the door, they crossed the street. Turning around the corner, they arrived at, the main drag. A few feet down the street, was a coffee shop, but, it was closing. Merrick looked around, discovered a deli, across the street, and guided her to it.

She ordered a mild coffee and he ordered a hot chocolate, no whipped cream. They sat with their drinks watching the street life, outside the window.

"This is charming," she said, overwhelmed with the newness of it all, plus feeling better, that they were not in the car.

"Yes, Calistoga is an old water town, with many spas and water holes."

America was a new country compared to Egypt, but America, was where she wanted to be. These old buildings were relatively old for a two hundred year old country.

The memory of structures that are thousands of years old, made her smirk. The present was richer, fuller. What Americans have done with their country, was amazing in such a short time.

"How are ya?" asked Merrick.

"I was a little car sick, actually," she offered. "I am really well now, though. And you?"

"Why didn't you tell me you were car sick?"

"Because it was not a big deal. I am fine, now."

"Now, that I'm not driving," he said, concerned.

"I am fine, really. Sorry I brought it up, even."

She looked at his worried expression.

"Really I am fine. How sweet. How are you doing?"

"I couldn't be happier," he said, seriously. "Your capacity for life, amazes me. You approach everything with so much vigor and wonder. As if everything you do, is for the first time." He watched her for a minute. "Like a child," he finished.

"Nice," she said, grinning, "now, I am childish."

"Not childish, like a child, with an open heart, and a fresh look, at everything. You are not tainted with regrets, and what could have been."

"No use," she said, flippantly. Then noticing how serious he was, she said, "Nothing is gained by bitterness. It only bites the one practicing it, in the ass."

She reached for her coffee and looked at his eyes. They were shining with tears.

"When I was going through divorce, my husband, bless his heart," she said, rolling her eyes, at the mention of her past marriage, "sent me and the girls to a psychiatrist, for evaluation. Well, court ordered, since he claimed, that I was really bad for my girls."

Sipping her coffee, she waved her left hand, in explanation.

"The psychiatrist saw me, then each daughter alone, then both together, then all three of us, together. Then, he sent the girls out of his office, and talked to me."

Taking a deep breath, she held her cup between her cold hands.

"I am not trying to make myself sound great or anything, but he told me, that my daughters did not have any bitterness, and that is directly attributed to me."

177

She raised her cup in the air, in a mock, self toast.

Taking her hand, Merrick, held it tightly.

"I have been through many sessions during the divorce. I have been to an alcohol Counsellor, I don't drink. I have peed in a cup at the rehab center, I do not do drugs. But my husband claimed, that I was taking drugs. I was taking, No-Doze, for my job during the night..." she sighed, trailing off.

"Anyhow, it is water under the bridge," she said, changing the subject. "I made it. It made me stronger and all the better for it."

"You got child support?"

"For one year," she laughed, "and Mr. Wonderful took off, went to Europe for a new job; leaving his daughters behind, so he would not pay child support."

Lifting her hand to stop him, as he started to say something else, she continued.

"The point is, it does not matter, what happened or did not happen, all is for a reason, and learning from it, is what the outcome is. If I hate my husband, that does not affect him one iota. It makes me bitter and angry. It does not affect him one bit."

Realizing the time while looking at his phone, he took her hand, pulling her off the seat.

"Time to go."

When they arrived at the Spa, he rented them towels, bought a bottle of water, then they walked, towards the dressing rooms.

"Just wait for me out here," he said, "I am sure you will get ready before me."

"Why? What are you doing in there?" she smirked, and slipped away, before he reached her.

The warm dressing rooms smelled of lavender and she

inhaled slowly, savoring the scent. Signs, everywhere, told you where to go, signs, also, told you, where not to trespass.

'Massage rooms, please be silent.'

'Do not enter, massage in progress'

She walked where the signs told her to be, where she took her clothes off. She wore her lame, black and gold bathing suit. A suit that held her big breasts, in, a sports bathing suit.

Looking in the mirror, she approved of what she saw, generally. Not bad, strong stomach, no six pack, by any stretch of the imagination, but strong and flat. She turned around, yeah well, no ass at all, never had one. She looked at her long sleek legs. Strong legs from years of rowing. Overall, not bad for a 47 years old grandmother, a GILF for sure. She smiled at her backside and taking her towel, walked out.

As predicted, she was earlier than he was. Waiting in the vestibule, looking at old spa pictures, of glory years gone by, hanging on the walls, she leisurely swung her arms.

Apparently, it had burnt in the past and was rebuilt several times. The pictures showed women, dressed in modest bathing suits, jumping into the large pool, like synchronized swimmer dancers, in a show.

Other pictures showed men and women in the water lounging and drinking martinis, while hanging over the bar, at the pool side.

"Here I am. Let's go for a soak."

Going through a gate into the pool area, they came upon four pools.

The first, a hexagon, very hot, 110 degrees and under a gazebo structure, for adults only.

The next one, was a medium one, with temperatures running at 98-104 degrees, under the open sky.

A lap pool with 75 degree temperature and four lanes and

four feet deep at its deepest.

A children's wading pool, with a waterfall, against the wall, warm and inviting.

Leading her to the open sky one, with medium temperature, they walked down the steps, into the water.

"I can't handle very hot water," he said, seriously. "My nerves don't handle much hotter than this."

Watching him walk down the steps, she wondered at his comments.

Wading to the deeper end of the pool, a little less than 6 feet, they huddled, in the corner. Gently pushing her in the corner, he leaned his back against her. Wrapping her arms and legs around him, she held him close.

"So, how long can we stay?" she whispered, in his ear.

"Two hours," he said, turning his head to her. "Seven till nine. We will be prunes by then."

She hugged him, closer.

"That is wonderful. Just enough to make it wonderful."

Not caring what time it was, she languidly soaked, when he turned to her. Placing one hand on either side of her shoulders, he whispered, "Look up, at the sky. Over my shoulder."

She raised her eyes to the brightest, full moon, just come up over the tree tops, beyond the pool.

She gasped in awe, tightening her hold on him.

All the days of being alone, all the days of wanting to share beauty, all the days of needing someone to express with, all those days are wrapped up in this glorious moment, of sharing.

"Where did you come from?" she whispered, in his ear.

"The moon," he said," I'm, an alien."

"Like me," she laughed. "I used to be an Alien Resident,

before I got my citizenship."

Clinging to each other, they kissed, passionately.

He laughed in her ear, gently, "Get a room, get a room. This is a family show."

She hid her head in his shoulder.

Time passed slowly, as they savored every moment. The moon was high above the trees now, and, in full view.

Looking over his shoulder, he said, "Time to go."

Turning, she lifted herself up out of the pool, and went to get their towels. Raising himself up, out of the water, she watched as he stripped as much of the water as he could off his hairy body. Passing his hands over his chest and back, then down his arms, then finally swiping his legs, he reached for the towel, she was holding open for him.

He smiled at her, noting that she kept waiting on him. Small things she did, small gestures of attention, that he was not used to.

Stepping towards her, hugging for a moment, they walked towards the dressing rooms.

She noticed the scales in the dressing room and stood on it. 152 pounds, no changes there.

As usual, she was showered, dressed and sitting in the waiting area, way before he came out.

As he was coming towards her, she turned to watch him. She loved to watch him. She did not steal glances at him, she openly, stared, at him.

Walking without hurry, he stepped with a slight sway, not arrogant, but relaxed. His arms swung ever so slightly, and he kicked one foot at a time, gently. Treading the earth gently, Merrick stepped, almost as if he did not want to disturb the ground he walked on.

Approaching her with a sweet smile, he leaned over to

kiss her.

The admittance wrist bands were cut off by the desk clerk. Then, they walked into the evening breeze.

He hugged her to him and she walked leaning into him, not for support, but for closeness.

If you consider the tension between them, uneventful, then the drive back to Sausalito, was boring. But, the tension seemed like a rubber band between them, taut at times, but looses and easy most of the time. When there was a tug, there was a release on the other end. A dance, between the two of them.

Arriving at her apartment, she was sleepy with the day's adventures, and he, was red eyed and groggy.

Reaching for the fireplace at the same time; together, they set up a fire. Undressing one another, they lay before it, talking.

Nothing earth shattering was said during this conversation. Nothing to solve world problems, or the Middle East crises. But, if either one needed to feel love, there was plenty to spill over.

Their lovemaking that night was soft, slow and easy. Neither one achieved orgasm in a physical sense, but they were elated with the experience, and the closeness.

Salma did not realize that a man could be satisfied with just being close to a woman, then, turn over and sleep; without physical release, in the traditional sense.

Turning, she faced the wall and started to dose off, when she felt him, come close. Spooning with her, he held her, tightly.

Another enigma in this man, he came close instead of wanting to be left alone, untouched. Intimacy, at its purest level.

Drifting off to sleep, they were entangled in each other.

BHAKTI BABE

*Every tree and plant in the meadow seemed to be
dancing, those which average eyes would see as fixed
and still*

- Rumi

Subject: Dance   *Mon Oct 13 2003*
To: Searcher   *From: The Scribe*

I wonder what you think of dance. I spent a few hours
last night dancing in worship.

It is an incredible form of worship that puts my whole
body into motion and devotion. I put some worship music on
and took off feeling the rhythm and beat and felt like flying.

My spirit was flying! My heart soared with love and rest.
I felt alive!

Salma

Subject: Re: Dance!   *Mon Oct 13 2003*
To: The Scribe   *From: Searcher*

>I wonder what you think of dance.<

Thank you for the great laugh this AM.

The only thing on my ahhhhuuuum, mind, is how
confining today's experience is. Having spent a glorious
day & expansive night with you, and then another good day
seeing how other artisans live… </sigh>

Having been sucked & licked into growth, today's

sprouting energy is forcibly confined in this damn pair of underwear! Loose & free isn't a controllable option today, thus the "need" to wear more fucking clothing than I'd like. Awareness of proper office attire is such a drag. The British maintain stiff upper lips; how energetically blazé of them…

>I felt alive!<

you little Bhakti Babe…

How is it that a Christian raised woman can be so in touch with her own Divinity? No guilt, no remorse, no damning Hell of pleasure. Yes, I've danced in ecstasy, Bhakti, Sufi, Kirtan - devotional sound is such a healing force.

Waaay too much heating Thai food, weekday night, cool fog, the beach we were on, stripped of clothes, and no music but the rhythms dancing in my head.

It didn't take long to find myself;

falling down on a blanket;

half laughing & crying;

the crisp fog reassembled my senses;

back to the boat for some hot tea.

-M

Subject: Re: Dance!   *Mon Oct 13 2003*
To: Searcher   *From: The Scribe*

I learned from the best teacher…Life! The joy of the knowledge of freedom is what allows me those un-guilty feelings of pleasure. It is called the peace that passeth all understanding. No guilt, no floggings, no hell fire, no damnation, no, no, no, no…..

I have suffered some for my beliefs but it is well worth it to me and what I have taught my children of freedom to live.

Your loving,

Salma

Subject: boring slide show   *Tue Oct 14 2003*
To: The Scribe   *From: Searcher*

Hello My Love,
Here's a little something I threw together in a real hurry.
It might be fun for you to look at, maybe ??!??
http://www.fantasmagorik.com/gallery/index.html
This is an automated slide show, with each slide advancing
every 10 seconds if left unattended. If you chose, you can
simply click through the thumbnails, or simply let it advance
on it's own.
— HOWEVER —
There's one slide you might not want to have showing on
a workplace screen for long, if so, scroll down the left side
thumbnail listing & click away to a different one. :-)
The questionable slide is called: racy_white.jpg
With love from a digital perspective,
Merrick

Subject: Ohhh My   *Tue Oct 14 2003*
To: The Scribe   *From: Searcher*

I didn't get much sleep in the early morning darkness…
more to follow!
All My Love,
Merrick

Subject: Re: Ohhh My   *Tue Oct 14 2003*
To: Searcher   *From: The Scribe*

Awaiting the rest with bated breath and racy thoughts…

can't help it, someone sent me a couple of photos of himself, like I need the help.
Salma

Subject: Re: boring slide show　　　　　　　*Tue Oct 14 2003*
To: The Scribe　　　　　　　　　　　　*From: Searcher*

>Thanks a fucking million....
Yes, I *am* happy to repay the "underwear" debt of yesterday. Oh, and looking wasn't required - it was your choice. :-)
LMAO,
Merrick

Subject: Re: boring slide show　　　　　　　*Tue Oct 14 2003*
To: Searcher　　　　　　　　　　　　*From: The Scribe*

You know what I imagined of course. Just the way I always slip myself under you, under your knee just the way you were laying on that beach.... yummy!
Your hungry,
Salma

Subject: Re: boring slide show　　　　　　　*Tue Oct 14 2003*
To: The Scribe　　　　　　　　　　　　*From: Searcher*

>laying on that beach.... yummy!
It was ****soooo**** hard to contain my internal laughter, as you came around to seeing the beach in a new light. Who needs a "movie", when real life is so, errr real!
Yes, that white picture was in the memory banks... The reason the phraseology sounded funny, we weren't including the all important word - personal.

Each of those photos was done alone that warm beach day, self timer on my 35mm camera...t ripod, or as in the gazing one, sitting on a rock.

Yep, just a boring slide show. :-)

-M

TRUE INSIGHT

Reason is like an officer when the king appears. The officer then loses his power and hides himself. Reason is the shadow cast by God; God is the sun.

- Rumi

Another e-mail from Francois that shed light on the way things were.

Subject: I have seen the light! Mon Oct 13 2003
To: Salma <The Scribe> *From: PepeCheeseHead*

Good morning, Salma!

Another marvelous one and are we not lucky to live in Marvelous Marin?

Thank you for your kisses back that found them being received by a New Man!

For... (and it is a VERY long story) I didn't actually "find a woman" (when I met her for coffee) as much as I encountered myself and discovered that I have been on the right track with myself (except for the need for the warmth of a woman) even though I didn't know it and I was resisting it (and whining to you about it!) all this time!

Because… I am thinking that perhaps I should just cool my jets for a while. And let the Universe do its magic on its own and for me to not be so desperate in my search. After all, the Universe brought me you without untold efforts on either of our parts! (This is a good thing.)

Perhaps then, I will be "chilling out" with this whole "warmth of a woman" business and look to simply enjoying being alive on days like this. And to being confident that all is as it should be. And to be content, for now, to marvel at you wonderful female creatures. To enjoy your sights and your sounds and your fragrances as I encounter them on the street or in a bookstore or at a cafe, celebrating your collective existence… and pretty much leaving it at that.

I am feeling that I am "one" with where I should be and I am VERY content with that.

Funny how it all worked out. And how your Holding Hands story was the linchpin of it all. For without that I would have remained clueless as to what I was attempting to deal with on the other side of my fence!

I am indebted to you as I find myself tres content ce jour!

How was YOUR weekend?

Gros bisous,

Francis aka Francois

COMMUNICATION

All day I think about it, then at night I say it. Where did I come from, and what am I supposed to be doing? I have no idea. My soul is from elsewhere, I'm sure of that, and I intend to end up there.
                                                        - Rumi

Subject: Simple Communication   *Tue Oct 14 2003*
To: The Scribe   *From: Searcher*

Good Morning My Love,

With a much happier sun rise guiding me forward and a totally DRAINED cell battery as we hung up, here's some of the detail that happened last night. As I explained on the phone this AM, the originating expression of this came to me in an energetically joyous fashion. I spent the following 2+ hours processing some of the details, including some of the "how might it work" stuff. I didn't get "enough sleep", but I know today will be easeful from the energy this gave me.

After some "Net" research to check its viability & soundness, here's the preliminary expression for you to contemplate also. If at any point a big red stop sign becomes visible for any reason, speak up - loudly!!

I'll tell you about my MacWorld / stockbroker / movie mogul experience the next time I see you. It's along these same lines in how it came about, and is another amazing chapter in my personal experience vault. That particular experience fell apart as the (you used the perfect word this morning) *strife* level become crazy. However, the original intent & the following events taught me so much. So without making you wait much longer, here's the result in *highly* preliminary text:

The domain, http://www.simplecommunication.org/ doesn't exist yet, so I just registered it for us. Now what shall we do with it? Here's one crazy thought wave:

= =

Simple Communication
(for Loving couples)
Postcard advertising mailer
Overview
Description
Objective

This should be as short as possible, fitting on the card; leaving enough room to fill in specific event details & the required US Postal regulations area for addressing & stamping.

- - - - - - -

Application Package

- - - - - - -

Full size color brochure
(envisioned as one double-sided letter sheet)
Includes full details of the card's basics above:
Overview
Description
Objective

—

One page application - with joint signatures

—

Interview & Survey Form, w/sealable envelope - Woman

—

Interview & Survey Form, w/sealable envelope - Man

—

Addressed envelope for the application & forms for easy return.

—

Side Note: This could also be offered to Gay & Lesbian couples, however with so much less experience, I'm hesitant to consider such today.

- - - - - - -

This overtly Oral workshop was envisioned as a Sat/Sun weekend training retreat; in communication, sexuality, and sacred space. It will be easy to do at the many places like Harbin Hot Springs, a place where naked self acceptance is the norm. However, the preliminary vision wasn't of open nakedness on the part of the participants. Emotional safety is the desired experience, stretching anyone beyond where they feel safe, unacceptable.

With a pick-up truck & enclosed trailer, it's possible to deliver on site a unique experience to the participants. I'll let you know more about this when I can verbally tell you about a drum & dance workshop I participated in.

Sat Morning

Registration

Sat Mid-Morning

Opening remarks, then split into male & female groups for bold communication

Return as a group to reacquaint, then give just enough time to process as couples

Lunch - catered buffet, group seating, yet couple flexible

Sat Mid - Afternoon

Juicy demos for the group

Dinner - catered buffet again

Sat Evening
Assembly of Sacred Spaces
Sun Morning/Afternoon
Brunch Buffet
Gather as a group to discuss what happened...
- - - - - - -

The new web address above (not fully functional yet) has the ability to handle all forms of web enabled communications, including email lists & member forums. A growing entity around personal training & empowerment is only one of many possibilities.

Anyway, it's a simple thought. A project like this, or any other, will bring us closer, continuously - or frighteningly, could become a wedge between us...

With Love, and not quite enough sleep,
Your Crazy Man,
Merrick

Subject: Re: Simple Communication   *Tue Oct 14 2003*
To: Searcher   *From: The Scribe*

> Anyway, it's a simple thought. A project like this, or any other, will bring us closer, continuously - or frighteningly, could become a wedge between us...<

WOW! Nothing simple about that thought! Nothing simple about that project. Nothing simple about our communication either.... lol. Not impossible, just not simple!

Merrick, you know that I am a Christian, I have had an enlightening experience where God showed me. That is the basis of my life, the basis of my whole faith.

Now, is that going to bring a wedge between us? Is it going to be a barrier?

The reason you see love in me is because of my relationship with the person of God. The One who manifested Himself to me openly and lovingly.

I love the project... preliminarily, I love it! Now, I have to take it and pray. Believe me when I tell you that nothing would make me happier than to start a project with you because you are right, it would bring us closer and that is my goal. On the other hand, I would not pick up a straw off the ground if I thought it would offend my faith...so, I pray!

Many projects have split couples apart. Usually the culprit is pride, want, and selfishness. I have learned over the years that my place as a woman is beside my Man. I was not made of a bone in his head so that he would not rule over me, not a bone of his foot, so he would not trample over me, but from his side so that I could walk hand in hand beside him, loving and cherishing him.

On that note, I have also learned that when a man is loved with that unconditional love that only a woman can offer, he can grow spiritually and emotionally. She becomes softer and more loving as he becomes stronger and more capable of life. That creates harmony and an ability to go through tragedy and joy with equilibrium... together.

God has taught me to be a woman. I was waiting for a man to allow it. Are you him?? I know the answer, do you??

With all my love,
Salma

Subject: A new direction!　　　　　　　　　*Tue Oct 14 2003*
To: Searcher　　　　　　　　　　　　　*From: The Scribe*

I need to share with you something that happened a few months ago Merrick.

I was praying about direction in my life for some reason..., anyhow! I clearly heard inside me that I will not be doing my job for long. Not specifically when or how it will end but that I will not be doing it for the rest of my life.

Another project for me. And it involves people. It is a training camp for women Merrick. A training facility not built anywhere, it is just anywhere there is a need.

It is a two week program in any state, any city or town. I get to go there and meet the 12 women who will enroll for it. The purpose is to teach them a purpose driven life which involves spiritual, physical and emotional guidance. How to be women, loving, warm, kind and be who they are in God.

Proposing what you did is so in synch with that, that it blew my mind away. The schedule that you set in your note was so familiar and so similar. I am so blessed! And, I do not have to do it alone Merrick. I have a partner who shares the same love for people and their well being… I am blown away!

I am overwhelmed!

Your adoring woman,

Salma

Subject: Re: A new direction!   *Tue Oct 14 2003*
To: The Scribe   *From: Searcher*

>I am overwhelmed!<

Which is why I didn't go any deeper in asking about last night's prayers. I knew enough from your answer to continue with what happened for me last night. Sharing with you the way it feels, without any additional feedback from you, was important to me.

Merrick

DECISIONS

Everyone sees the unseen in proportion to the clarity of his heart, and that depends upon how much he has polished it. Whoever has polished it more sees more - more unseen forms become manifest to him.

- Rumi

Subject: Desperate Agony   *Wed Oct 15 2003*
To: The Scribe   *From: Searcher*

Dearest Love,

With tears flowing down my cheeks this morning, oh yes, I knew what I was doing yesterday afternoon, just as I *needed* you this AM. Your voice being the only physical connection for me in this moment of desperate wanting.

The energy of the oar carried me up the steps yesterday, panting, heaving; the shorts remaining damp, with the addition of the stair induced sweat. Oh yes, the happy tears were known, the aromas available to fill your emotions & create such painful pleasures. The pleasures I enjoyed while stroking & creating my present.

Salma, there's no need to worry. Pragmatism is a horrible infliction, asking what needs done to move myself forward, and keeping me from fucking in a most foolish & frantic moment. I didn't give you those fabric flowers to tease. They're pacifiers to satiate the senses, while I'm still too damn distant.

I want to make love when & as it feels right, not because

there's a brief & stolen moment. I'm doing what I can for the much longer term ahead. If my wants are met, it will be with you by my side, filling you with myself.

My emotional loins ache, because this Thursday, Friday & Saturday are days & nights of seemingly endless work. I'm going to be doing what I must, all the while, with you too distant.

I want to Live like artists; open, simple, free.

I want to Love like animals; open, simple, free.

Dearest, I am not "waiting too long", for I've wanted you in my life from the day I stepped on the spiritual path.

Drying the tears as work beckons yet again,

Merrick

Subject: Re: Simple Communication   *Tue Oct 14 2003*
To: Searcher   *From: The Scribe*

> With a pick-up truck & enclosed trailer, it's possible to deliver on site a unique experience to the participants.<

You have no idea what that does to me just thinking about it. Thinking of being with you, sharing our life and love with others, letting them know why and how it works.

We do not know that it works do we?? We know that it has the potential to work. Nothing will be clear until we are truly together, the daily grind, the laundry, the cooking, the cleaning, the bills, the responsibilities.... etc. things that are life! How it is all handled between us, two separate entities yet one under love.

To convey that joy we have to know where we stand first. I am confident of my end.... :-) I love you with all my heart and soul. My needs come after yours because I love you. My focus is on you because I love you. My desire is for you to be happy and fulfilled no matter what the price because I love you. My heart is at your disposal because I love you. My trust is complete in you because I love you......

    Should I go on??

    Salma

Subject: Re: Simple Communication   *Tue Oct 14 2003*
To: Searcher   *From: The Scribe*

    > Overview: A time for couples to get closer.

    >Description

    >This weekend will give you the opportunity to explore each other freely without restraint. It is a guided tour into the possibilities of your relationship.

    >Objective: Better communication for a joy filled life.

    Comments? What do you think? Would it work??

    It's a start!

    Salma

Subject: wildly tame   *Tue Oct 14 2003*
To: The Scribe   *From: Searcher*

    sandals, shorts, t-shirt, out the door to Sansome, up the Filbert St. stairs to Coit Tower, down again through Levi Plaza, Jamba Juice & bread for lunch, restlessly energized, I am looking forward too...

    -M

Subject: Re: wildly tamed   *Tue Oct 14 2003*
To: Searcher   *From: The Scribe*

    Thanks for the visual! What are you trying to do?? It is already done!! I find myself floating to where you are to watch over you and watch you. I imagine your cold room, the table you work at, the environment.

I imagine the freedom we could experience together without the constraints of these jobs we hold now. The possibilities are endless. The time is unlimited. The love boundless.

mmmm… mmmmm…. mmmmmmm…. yummy!

So, she decided that things were not getting warm enough, things were not, heating enough, as if! She decided, that she should start writing stories, to him. Stories of passion. Stories, made up, of her desire, and imagination. As if things were not progressing too fast and too hot, she decided, to add salt and pepper.

If Anais Nin could come up with stories that tantalized her audience, she Salma, could do the same, with her lover.

So, she wrote to him, again.

One of Salma's favorite writers was always Anais Nin. Writing to pleasure her clients, was what Nin did, and, what she achieved was remarkable.

With that in mind, Salma conjured up Nin's spirit recreating some of her weird imaginations. Drawing on her feelings for Merrick, she proceeded to write him stories of fantasy and lust.

Again, a new Salma in the making. Here she went, doing something completely out of the ordinary for this man. Meanwhile, he never asked for this. Why, then, was she driven to do this?

'Anais Nin, you inspired me,' thought Salma, as she sat to write.

Subject: Passion!   *Tue, Oct 14 2003*
To: Searcher   *From: The Scribe*

She tries to be quiet during the night when she wakes up. She tries not to move or roll over or anything…but alas, she does not succeed, she needs to look. She turns her head to watch the sleeper. It does not take long for his eyes to flutter open and a smile.

She dives under the covers to reach for her prize. She inhales him, fills her senses with his sleepy aroma. She pushes her mouth, tongue and nose into him to savour every spec of him. She rubs her face into him, smearing herself with his juices and his sleep sweat.

Then her tongue laps at the liquid, tasting. She reaches into the crevices, the nooks and the crannies between his thighs. She pushes her tongue and lips under his sack and licks around. She pushes against that soft spot under his sack down………

She slides her tongue down that beautiful flesh. She inhales deeply at the surprise of his taste, it is private, it is personal, it is him, only him, his taste, his smell, him, only!

She could feel his urgency now and he lifts his hips off the bed. He holds her head and pushes himself down on her mouth and tongue and she pushes back. The urgency is heightening and he wraps his fingers in her hair and pulls her to his cock and she swallows it.

He calls out her name and she wets herself. He calls her

name again and pushes himself deeper into her soft cavern, hungry mouth. She is insatiable when it comes to his cock, she cannot have enough. She tried to hold back as long as she could to keep him wanting, but she does not want him wanting, she wants him satisfied and pleasured.

ALLOWING LIFE

Move outside the tangle of fear-thinking.
Live in silence."
                                   - Rumi

Shopping at Mollie's Market in Sausalito, Salma picked up a ripe mango, a box of strawberries that smelled just right and plump blueberries. When she got home, she washed the fruit, noting the beautiful colors.

Laying each piece in the box, imagining what it would be like for Merrick, to open the lid, finding everything arranged, with care and love.

Slicing the strawberries, she laid, the pieces down, closely. The strawberries were fire engine red, and shining. The mango was ripe and she could smell its strong aroma. She peeled and then cut it into long thin strips, and lay them beside the strawberries. The orange color of the mango glowed, in the early morning light. Lastly, she put the round blueberries on the third section of the box and saw how the blue, toned everything down, making it, stand out.

From her seat on the deck, she watched Tiburon, which glowed in the evenings, at sunset. The sun's reflection was in the windows and glass; across the water, shining, like gold, shimmered in the water.

Sighing, she rested back against the door jamb, watching the beauty surrounding her. Yes, love did make everything more pronounced, more beautiful and more exotic. She smiled to herself thinking of Merrick, how kind and attentive he was to her.

Dressing in gym clothes, the athlete, drove to the Marin Rowing Club. She had a 'date' with one of the women there, to use the ERG, and exercise. They did this together to keep their skills and strength up.

Rowing, was one of her passions.

Training on the ERG, she thought, she felt someone behind her; watching. It felt unnerving and yet comforting. It was too early for someone to be up at this hour, if they were not rowing or training, five am, is not a time to lurk around, unless you are up to something bad, or …. She turned her head, as she pulled the chain towards her, and sure enough, there was Merrick, leaning against one of the columns.

"What are you doing here?" she asked, stunned.

"Just came by to see what you do so early in the morning."

He was smiling, and his blue eyes sparkled, even in the darkness of the morning.

The other few athletes who were there looked on, curiously. Everyone knew she was single. Her rower friend, turned to one of the guys and said, "Where is your wife, this morning, Jack?"

"In bed," said Jack, not amused, "where she belongs."

"She is not here, to see what you're doing, nor encourage you, I see."

"Neither, is your husband," he said, laughing, finally.

It was true, men did not like to be shown up, by other

men, some locker room thing, Merrick had once explained to Salma. When a man did something 'nice' it put pressure on the other men, to do the same. They do not like or appreciate that, at all.

She had laughed when Merrick told her that. Yet, remembered that her own mother, had once mentioned, that when she did 'nice' things for her husband, in front of other people, "the women will grow to hate you, since they do not want their husbands to expect the same from them". She sighed thinking of her mother.

Not wanting to interrupt her training, she kept it up, did what she intended to do, when she first got there; albeit with less concentration, and a lot more distraction.

After 30 minutes they were done, then it was time to go for shower, coffee and work, in that order.

Merrick took her hand, as they walked out to their cars. Ending up at Chuck's Coffee, in Bon Air Plaza. The coffee was strong and thick. Merrick was obviously not a coffee drinker and Salma just drank, Moonbeam.

The morning passed swiftly, and they had to part. He went to work, and she to hers. It was a sweet sensation, knowing that someone wanted to be where you were, even, when you were not paying him any attention, just to be there, with you.

Before they left she handed him the box of fruit.

Smiling at the memory of it, she hugged herself wondering how long such caring lasted, and how she could take a hold of it, and not let go.

'Just keep doing what you do. Just keep being who you are,' she told herself. Long term, means being who you are, and not someone else, to trap another.

Smiling at the constant conversations and constant

reminders to herself, she shook her head. If she was someone else doing that, she would have told that person to, shut up, and cut it out, already.

Past experiences taught her, that being someone else, to please another, did not last very long. She had never done it personally, but knew so many who did, friends and lovers who would start off, being someone they imagined themselves to be. And, as time went by, grew tired of the charade, and went back to their original self.

Now that self may have been lovely and endearing to someone, but, it was usually, not what the partner, was expecting, since they, were introduced, to the wrong persona.

Chortling at the way her mind was rushing, with thoughts and ideas, Salma, clutched herself, all day. Something inside her was softening. Feeling the shell, she put around her, to avoid hurt, breaking away, she felt unnerved. The shell of expectations was coming apart.

Expect nothing, so you would not be hurt; was a terrible motto. She had lived by it for years, and now, she could see that it was crumbling, under the careful attention of Merrick.

Subject: Allowing Life!   *Wed Oct 15 2003*
To: Searcher   *From: The Scribe*

Merrick
Thank you my darling for allowing life to move forward.

I am overwhelmed with your openness and your love. I appreciate the things you do for me and the things you allow me to do with you.

You are truly unique in acceptance and giving.

I am sorry that I did not pick up the phone when you called. I like to be available to you whenever you want me. Unfortunately today I had to go rowing and I cannot take my phone with me, so yes, it was turned off when you called.

I have had too much energy and if I would have come to work in this shape it would have been a rough day for my coworkers :-).

I love you Merrick with all my heart. You make me skip instead of walk. You make me laugh instead of just smile. You make me smile when I could be frowning. Thank you again for being you.

Your,
Salma

Subject: Re: Allowing Life!   *Wed Oct 15 2003*
To: The Scribe   *From: Searcher*

>I am sorry that I did not pick up the phone when you called.<

LOL - the moment you said "rowing", I knew what day it was, but not until then.

I have had too much energy and if I would have come...

How much did you say a proper shell was again???

If energy isn't channeled appropriately; flames transform...

Vespoli ??, Hudson ??, Durham ??, BBG??

Home located next to the lake: priceless.

Merrick

Subject: Re: Desperate Agony   *Wed Oct 15 2003*
To: Searcher   *From: The Scribe*

My Merrick,

Your need for me is only surpassed by my need for you.

Jan, my friend, is coming on Friday and Saturday and will leave on Sunday some time. That is probably good since I will be busy while you are away.

Again... I will wait! Do what you must Merrick! Be pragmatic, it makes sense even then. I have been accused of pragmatism and in it I see you as a good end result.

Stolen moments of love-making are good if the alternative is nothing. I am happy with that if I can be with you and near you. You have no idea.

I slept with your scent around me last night. Thank you! Yes, it pacified me... thank you. I cried a little for I ache for your presence, your flesh, your voice, your hair, your skin, your face, your everything. I ache for your weight, your abandon, your surprise, your motion. I ache for your giving of yourself to me. I adore you.

Take your time Merrick. I am here.

Delayed gratification... something I am learning at an old age. When the time comes for us, it will be precious and we will know and remember how it felt when we were apart.

My only regret is that I was not available to you this morning. I am sorry...when I heard your message, I cried! The sunrise was not the same without your voice.

I ache to hold you Merrick. Come home to me.

Salma

Subject: Diagnosis = Crazy   *Wed Oct 15 2003*
To: The Scribe   *From: Searcher*

Spiritual Tinnitus

About 18 months ago, a rather boring lecture had me & my flogging mind wandering off. I was sitting in a yoga studio faintly listening to the instructor, a good friend working away in the next room. I heard a noise emanate from the adjacent room, and the next thing I heard was a loud ringing in my right ear. It's been there ever since. When I'm "busy" or sleeping, it seems to vanish. At any other time, it's like a constantly buzzing fly; it's been a rather annoying reality.

I then meet one wild woman on a bridge, and ever since, the ringing in my right ear has decreased in volume & the pitch has become noticeably higher. To add even more oddness, whenever I'm with her, the ringing becomes so faint as to disappear completely.

The yogis say whatever this is I'm experiencing is a blessing.

To me, it's crazy.

-M

Subject: Re:Rowing!   *Wed Oct 15 2003*
To: Searcher   *From: The Scribe*

Thank you for checking out those sites for me. I do appreciate it. There are some very good and interesting prices in there and maybe instead of that motorcycle, I can actually get myself a sculling shell... that would be great actually.

Near a lake... wow... and enough land to build a barn with high ceilings to make a studio for photography and painting or maybe stained glass work.

Food for thought!

Salma

Subject: Bzzzzzt, adoring amazement   *Thu Oct 16 2003*
To: The Scribe   *From: Searcher*

Hello My Love,

The treat of a ride was a delight, the tasty chocolate & coffee, a morning necessity!!!!!

I don't know how you know each time, but this morning has been insane.

1st a dead scanner on an important machine.

2nd, a second machine with a scanner has major trouble.

Easy enough, rip the scanner off the major trouble machine, replacing the dead one - and poof one working machine...

However, the major trouble has been a hectic nightmare. Nothing was working on it... It took me almost 2 hours to get the machine to recognize itself again. I'm now copying off all of it's data, will soon reinitialize the hard drive, install a new operating system, and only then will I know if it's not a hardware issue...

Your drink of adornment has been a GREAT treat. Besides being a delicious indulgence, it's kept me moving at a pace that's not normally done... Lunch soon, and then maybe a short break from the hectic-ness...

Thank you, thank you, thank you!

In shock again at your forethought,

Merrick

Subject: Thank you!   *Thu Oct 16 2003*
To: Searcher   *From: The Scribe*

It is rather simple! I happen to truly love you. Thank you for seeing the sunrise with me, Merrick. I adore you!

My head was still up .... :-)
Salma

Subject: Re: Diagnosis = Crazy   *Thu Oct 16 2003*
To: Searcher   *From: The Scribe*

I am not sure what to say...I read it yesterday and am still not sure what to say ...I am humbled by being with you.
Salma

Subject: Re: Diagnosis = Crazy   *Thu Oct 16 2003*
To: The Scribe   *From: Searcher*

>I am not sure what to say...I read it yesterday and am still not sure what to say ...<
If you knew what to say to this, I'd probably collapse. Fully realized sages would have trouble with this question of merging faith & biology. Not to worry. I didn't pose it for you to find an answer. It was an observation that has my eyes open...
Love,
Merrick

Subject: Re: Bzzzzt, adoring amazement   *Thu Oct 16 2003*
To: Searcher   *From: The Scribe*

Do you remember me telling you that my daughter always laughs and tells me that my whole life is an acid trip??? :-)
I walk every day in the Spirit. I live life without guilt, without guile and without strife.
The only way to know if one is walking in the Spirit is to see the fruit. A dead tree yields nothing...a tree that is alive will have branches and green leaves and even the birds of the

sky will take cover under it. A loving tree with living waters.

I love you Merrick…I already miss you.

Salma

Subject: Re: Bzzzzt, adoring amazement   *Thu Oct 16 2003*
To: The Scribe   *From: Searcher*

>It is rather simple! I happen to truly love you.<

LOL

Ya but - how could you know my day NEEDED the buzzzzt from coffee?

Oh, and the "shakiness" of the caffeine didn't go away for almost 2 hours - and at this very moment, without any additional nourishment in my system, there's the slightest of headaches as a remnant.

Lovingly,

Merrick

Subject: Re: Bzzzzt, adoring amazement   *Thu Oct 16 2003*
To: The Scribe   *From: Searcher*

A loving tree with living waters.

How about spreading your loving tree & its living waters?

-M

Subject: Re: Bzzzt, adoring amazement   *Fri Oct 17 2003*
To: Searcher   *From: The Scribe*

You forget one important element…People have to come to the tree and be under it to pick the fruit and to enjoy the shade…:-)

Salma

Subject: Re: picking labor   *Fri Oct 17 2003*
To: The Scribe   *From: Searcher*

>People have to come to the tree and be under it to pick the fruit and to enjoy the shade...:-) <

Well Crap. Just where do you think I've been these weeks?

Picking fruit, lifting boxes, working my ass to the bone...

I haven't been lounging in the shade doing nothin', that's for sure.

Taking a break for a moment, my back a bit sore again, getting hungry, most everything aching really. The amount of crap impressive, the past glaring into places I'd tried to leave in the past.

I'm off to the store, the hole in my stomach needing something.

uuurrrrrrrgh,

-M

Subject: Re: picking labor   *Fri Oct 17 2003*
To: Searcher   *From: The Scribe*

LOL!!!!

I would help if you let me...I would be hauling, lifting and picking for you so you would not have to hurt your back.

I love you!

Salma

Subject: Perhaps   *Fri Oct 17 2003*
To: The Scribe   *From: Searcher*

Dearest,

There's space opening up from within these many boxes. As I gaze into each one, the contents are usually cast aside in an uneasy moment.

How could I use this going forward?

The past keeps the present from being,

the future from advancing. Perhaps.

-M

Subject: Re: Perhaps   *Fri Oct 17 2003*
To: Searcher   *From: The Scribe*

> The past keeps the present from being, the future from advancing. Perhaps.<

Choices!

Is the past worth keeping?? If it is, then you should. If it will make you happy then you should.

Looking back holds us rooted in our place and yes, does not allow us to go forward.

I am sorry that it is a sad time! Ending things usually is. I understand.

Whatever you decide Merrick, I will support your decisions. I love you and wish I could hold you.

Salma

Subject: Re: Perhaps   *Sun Oct 19 2003*
To: Searcher   *From: The Scribe*

I am so glad you will "likely" be here Sunday. I miss you.

Salma

Subject: Re: Perhaps   *Sat Oct 18 2003*

To: The Scribe   *From: Searcher*

>Is the past worth keeping?? If it is, then you should. <
The past is never worth clutching, it is not life being lived!
>Whatever you decide<
I decide to continue cleaning, making space for infinite possibilities. I may one day write of this experience, but for now, I'm busy creating it.
I'll likely be there Sunday night...
In Love (and dusty / crusty remnants),
Merrick

Subject: Good Morning!   *Mon Oct 20 2003*
To: Searcher   *From: The Scribe*

I just left you a few minutes ago and I already miss your beautiful smile and miss holding you.
Our start is slow...I could have held you longer and loved you longer. I cannot wait till tonight to hold you and make love to you.
Your adoring,
Salma

Subject: Shower!   *Mon Oct 20 2003*
To: Searcher   *From: The Scribe*

I felt abandoned.... :-)
Not really...just missed you in the shower and was not sure if you did not want to come in since it was so early....
siiigggghhhhhhh!
Kisses,
Salma

Subject: *Re: Shower!*   Mon Oct 20 2003
To: *The Scribe*   From: Searcher

>was not sure if you did not want to come in<
LOL...

It wasn't early. I stayed out on better behavior. I didn't cross the doorway into the streaming warmth of temptation. I surely didn't want to be the topic of "why she's late" around the water cooler today!!!

As it was:

It was all I could do to keep the shower from being a rather large delay. However, lounging in the ease of it all, I wasn't exactly early to the office either. I caught a number 10 bus, which took me to the ferry building. Having waited just a few minutes, the boat took me through the golden glow of this sparkling morning.

Walking from the Ferry Terminal, I made it into the office with only a couple minutes to spare. This journey was NOT like my lengthy Sonoma County bus ride at all. I'm breathing easier today, my head swimming in a sea of little waves.

With Love,

Merrick

SHOWER AND PAIN

If in thirst you drink water from a cup, you see God in it. Those who are not in love with God will see only their own faces in it.

- Rumi

Subject: Morning Thought!   *Tue Oct 21 2003*
To: Searcher   *From: The Scribe*

Wilson was blind for 7 years. One day he woke up with terrible pains in his eyes. The pain seared through the back of his eyes like lightening and suddenly he could see his dog laying at his feet. He was astounded. He then lifted his head up and could see his wife for the first time in 7 years and kept looking at the woman who loved him all this time.

A few hours later things got hazy and it was clear white liquid and he could not see again.

When he went to the doctor, she told him that the optic nerve is attaching itself to his retina and she did not have an explanation for it.

Someone asked Wilson: Do you look forward to the pain?

His eyes sparkled as he said emphatically.... Yes.

There is a certain clarity that comes with pain. We see through the haze of the pain the beauty that we would have missed otherwise.

Salma

Subject: Re: Shower!   Tue Oct 21 2003
To: Searcher   From: The Scribe

My time with you is so precious to me.

I thought about what you said last night about energy and expending it regarding sexual release. I have many questions and much I want to understand and learn about that and other things you mention.

Whether you achieve release or not is of no consequence. Not because I do not care but because I do. I want you to do and be whatever you want to be and do when we are together. Coming or not is not the issue, it is my mouth on every part of your body, to love and to heal. And that is why I ask before I do anything. It is not because I am unaware of what you want or need sometimes but it is confirmation.

I lead my life like a child. I approach life and living in a much simpler way I suppose. When my body needs nourishment, I give it. When it needs release I let it. When it needs energy release I exercise. I simply live without thinking.

I have realized that God has allowed me time to live and leads me into this living thing with ease and without complications. No taboos and no circumference, just life! I do not hold back and I let myself go with abandon.

I love you Merrick, so much! I find my time with you an energizing time that fills me with awe and wonder at the beauty of life. Makes me want to be a better person, makes me kinder to the world (but I have told you that before).

With all my love,
Salma

Subject: Is that you? Earth? Is it 1959?   Tue Oct 21 2003
To: Searcher   From: The Scribe

Those of you born under the influence of the Chinese Astrology Element of Earth are wise, serene and prudent, firmly rooted in your morals, ethics and responsibilities. Led by logic rather than emotion, you seek to plan your life as far out in advance as possible, to expect the unexpected and control your destiny down to the last detail. Your disciplined reserve — which can come across as true grace if you work it right — garners you respect and admiration.

You're so bound by logic and dependent upon controlling your situation that you have a fear of the unknown. Consequently, you question your instincts, distrusting even your most cherished dreams and seeing your whims as frivolous distractions. Don't be a stick in the mud, Earth Signs; share your wisdom and your peace of mind with a needy world.

Now, she was writing like him. What the hell was wrong with that picture? Chinese astrology indeed! Live and learn.

Subject: Is that you? Earth? Is it 1959?   *Tue Oct 21 2003*
To: The Scribe   *From: Searcher*

<Those of you born under the influence of the Chinese Astrology Element of Earth<

Nope. 1960 = Metal

Those of you born under the influence of the Chinese Astrology element of Metal are determined, self-reliant and forceful. You enjoy the good life and all it has to offer — luxury, comfort and freedom, especially. You're like a reclusive film star: you want the acclaim, but you also want to be left alone. You create your own success, building your desired destiny with single-minded focus. Others look up to you in awe of your commanding, confident presence.

While you Metal individuals are strong and virtuous, you can be a bit set in your ways. No arm-wrestling with the metallic ones, either; they might break that appendage in two! You can be a stern taskmasters as well, demanding the most from yourself and those you love.

I especially espouse the belief in needing maximum luxury, comfort, and freedom! :-)))))

And I'm just like George Clooney, Jennifer Lopez, and Britney Spears too!!!

What a crock...

Merrick

Subject: Is that you? Earth? Is it 1959?   *Tue Oct 21 2003*
To: Searcher   *From: The Scribe*

LOL!

How true! What a crock! And I am selfish and seek my own pleasure and am unfaithful...how sad! I am the fire monkey...sheeesh!

Salma

Subject: How much is enough!   *Tue Oct 21 2003*
To: Searcher   *From: The Scribe*

Charlie from Techtronics was here today to fix an IT problem we have had with a monitoring cable to the 3D computer. We were chatting and he asked me if I was going to be in St. Luke's for the first case. I replied that indeed I would be there. He asked if they paid me well to be there, since I work in Marin, I should be paid lots to go there.

I laughed and told him that I get paid the same. He told me that it was ridiculous and that they should appreciate me and pay me more. I laughed it off. He insisted to which I replied that I was very content with what I am making. It is enough!

He told me and very seriously....."It is never enough!" He was completely serious too.

Sigh!
Salma

Subject: Re: How much is enough!   *Tue Oct 21 2003*
To: The Scribe   *From: Searcher*

>"It is never enough!<
Sigh!
</too much on> **Insert** flaming RANT here! </too much off>
-M

Subject: Re: How much is enough!   *Tue Oct 21 2003*
To: Searcher   *From: The Scribe*

It made me sad because he is very wealthy. He owns a 9000 square foot home on a ranch in Tallahassee near, Bush. He is a decent man and has raised his sister, when he was only 25 and his sister was ten. He is sending her to college

now at 17, so he is a decent guy....I was sad!
Salma

>so he is a decent guy....I was sad!<
And he probably has a big truck too?
>>FIRST TEXAN: My ranch is so big it takes me all day
to drive across it. SECOND TEXAN: I had a truck like that
once.

This type of "never enough" mentality won't be driving
this brand new technology from Toyota:

http://www.toyota.com/prius-hybrid/

MPG = 60 highway, 51 city, 55 combined

I **REALLY** want this Hybrid Synergy Drive in my
new truck!!!

<sigh> patience grasshopper, patience <sigh>
Merrick

Good Morning my Darling,

How are you? I am sure that you are beat and tired to the
bone. I wish I could hold you and rock you. I wished I could
last night when you were so tired and sounded so weary.

But today, I hopped into the shower and saw your shaving
mirror and razor and smiled and it made my day. Little
pleasures! Little joys to make me smile and be happy.

I miss your mouth there, I miss your hand there and I
miss you there...in those secret places that make my body
reacts to with love and response. I never thought that I could

say that to a man, that I missed his mouth there but I do miss yours.

I wish you a wonderful day. I wish you a restful day. I wish you a pleasant day. I wish you everything you want on this foggy beautiful day.

Your lover,
Salma

Subject: Re: A blessed day coming your way!   *Thu Oct 23 2003*
To: The Scribe   *From: Searcher*

>Good Morning my Darling, How are you?<

Good morning (err, afternoon with the way it's going) to you as well???

The commute to SF was a looooooong 135 minute journey today. Traffic was rough the entire way, including the SF surface streets. Something is definitely not feeling right, both within whatever inner world exists as me & this outer manifestation too.

Today's Heart Quote seems to sum up the feeling pretty well:

"The great Western disease is, 'I'll be happy when. . . .' " he says. "When I get the money. When I get a BMW. When I get this job. Well, the reality is, you never get to when. The only way to find happiness is to understand that happiness is not out there. It's in here. And happiness is not next week. It's now."

— Marshall Goldsmith, executive coach

I can't say I'm "unhappy", and at the same time, am I really truly, down deep, happy Now? If I can't answer in an absolute positive manner, then maybe I'm not.

You are 100% correct, my body is feeling bone tired & sore too. Yesterday's 4:00 AM rising to 6:30 PM arrival back in Sonoma took a great deal from me. Each time something like this happens, my thoughts turn immediately to "why" do I continue doing this??

>I wish you everything you want on this foggy beautiful day.<

LOL!!!

Most everything I would "want" is not found in this doggedly determined existence of commuting & techno troubles. Refashioning my experience into something other than this, well, it seems like a challenge of nearly impossible proportions.

I've been thinking about this weekend, how I'm doing, and what your wants / needs might be. As of this moment, I'm thinking it best for you to take care of yourself, finding a "room" (if offered)...I'd still like to see you & the event, however, I'm not certain about what this might mean. I might want to arrive with a second car...??

Anyway, today, I'm mentally ambushed - so basing anything I'm doing from this space, probably unwise...

With Love,
Merrick

Subject: New Directions!   *Thu Oct 23 2003*
To: Searcher   *From: The Scribe*

God pushes us sometimes in directions that we are not comfortable with. Allowing us discontent so that we could move on. Allowing us the feeling of dissatisfaction so that we could go in new directions and move on with LIFE.

Life moves on and does not wait on anyone and things happen for a good reason. Discontent is built in us so that we could move forward and not get rooted in our "safe" zones

I wish you motion. I wish you happiness with or without me...

Salma

Subject: Re: New Directions!   *Thu Oct 23 2003*
To: The Scribe   *From: Searcher*

>Discontent is built in us so that we could move forward and not get rooted in our "safe" zones.<

I don't wish to be "safe", and at the same time, would certainly not want to be impaled by the stuff that's feeling secure...

No matter, the day is almost sunny around here - good enough reason to walk out into it, and get myself some lunch...

Motion???? Ha! Today, what I wish for is a warm, peaceful place to contemplate navel fuzz...

-M

Subject: Re: New Directions!   *Thu Oct 23 2003*
To: Searcher   *From: The Scribe*

> Today, what I wish for is a warm, peaceful place to contemplate navel fuzz...<

Then get to my apartment and rest and I will find another place to stay tonight.

Salma

Subject: Re: New Directions!   *Thu Oct 23 2003*
To: The Scribe   *From: Searcher*

>Then get to my apartment and rest and I will find

another place to stay tonight.<

What a cute response. However, evicting you to another place wouldn't be a peaceful solution to my personal sensibilities. What I was thinking of was a warm tropical beach, or creek side spot of green grass, basking in the sun, like some twisted guardian of fate...

-M

Subject: Re: A blessed day coming your way! Thu Oct 23 2003
To: Searcher *From: The Scribe*

> I can't say I'm "unhappy", and at the same time, am I really truly, down deep, happy Now? If I can't answer in an absolute positive manner, then maybe I'm not.<

Not unhappy... restless and getting ready. It is an uncomfortable feeling when we realize that what we have been doing for so long is not what we should have been or what we could have been doing.

It is a new beginning...it is something good... something positive... something new... something beautiful to look forward to... something for life ahead...

You are in the middle of it and it is hard to see that this feeling of "not right" is a good feeling for change. A feeling that comes with the dawning of major changes inside and out.

I changed my circumstances when I was living with my roommate because there was a need for that change to make room... remember?? Room for peace and for change and for what was coming new my way...

Life will continue with or without you but it is so much better with you in it.... :-)

Salma

Subject: Re: I love you Merrick!   *Thu Oct 23 2003*
To: The Scribe   *From: Searcher*

Earlier this week, I'd mentioned doing something else for "lodging" this weekend. If I'm to see you this weekend, and with my current state of tiredness, we might need two cars in Sacramento...I don't know. The reason I said what I did, was so that you'd have the opportunity to find a spot for yourself on Saturday night - regardless of how I might be doing...
 -M

Subject: Choices!   *Thu Oct 23 2003*
To: Searcher   *From: The Scribe*

> Yesterday's 4:00 AM rising to 6:30 PM arrival back in Sonoma took a great deal from me. Each time something like this happens, my thoughts turn immediately to "why" do I continue doing this??<
 Because you choose to! You could have stayed the night and you would not have had to arise at 4. I could have taken you in and brought you back...no sweat! I wanted to! You chose not to.
 Salma

Subject: I love you Merrick!   *Thu Oct 23 2003*
To: Searcher   *From: The Scribe*

I love you Merrick! Do as you will with that. I refuse to give up on you any time soon. Loving someone means understanding the times they are down and the times they are confused and the times they are tired.
 My only wish is that I could be with you in those times but that has to come from you since I am open to it. You have

to decide that.

You are not evicting me…it is my decision. In your last e-mail you suggested what I should do with myself and how I should take care of myself…thanks! I am very capable of making those decisions also. I deliberately make decisions, I do not let situations drag me along.

Salma

Subject: Re: I love you Merrick!   *Thu Oct 23 2003*
To: Searcher   *From: The Scribe*

I want to be with you regardless of whether we have sex or not. I want to spend time with you…not just have sex with you. You can be tired with me….I can handle that too.

Salma

Subject: Re: I love you Merrick!   *Thu Oct 23 2003*
To: The Scribe   *From: Searcher*

>I want to be with you regardless of whether we have sex or not.<

LOL, this isn't about sex - but what I might need to restore myself to some resemblance of "normal". That might not be spending two days at what could most likely be a very HOT lake location…

-M

Subject: Amazing!   *Thu Oct 23 2003*
To: Searcher   *From: The Scribe*

It continues to amaze me! People continue to amaze me! You know what you need to do. You feel it! You sense it! You see it! You avoid it!

I hope that something good and peaceful opens your eyes to the wonders of a serene life without fear and self-imposed struggle.

Salma

COMMUNICATION BREAKDOWN

The Eternal looked upon me for a moment with His eye of power, and annihilated me in His being, and become manifest to me in His essence. I saw I existed through Him.

- Rumi

Subject: Re: weekend's rain   *Mon Oct 27 2003*
To: Searcher   *From: The Scribe*

>Since leaving my phone in your car, I've been given the chance to think as well. Today, I'm not liking what's appearing. It's not good when we don't bring out the absolute best in each other, but when it degrades into this, I'm not feeling well.<

I am not sure I understand.... Please explain to me. I would have been happy to drop off the phone anywhere you wanted. I would have even brought it to you at the end of the day somewhere in between our houses....hmmm...I am not sure I understand.
Salma

What in the world was this man talking about? Since leaving his telephone in her car, Merrick seemed unhinged. Salma tried several times to make heads or tails of what he attempted to explain to her but never came up with any coherent explanation.

Wondering constantly what someone else was thinking was exhausting. Hoping to appease someone, without understanding the real problem, proved to be impossible. An impossible task by an old woman, who could not possibly begin to recognize, the pain a man would be going through.

Words went back and forth between the two lovers. Some were comforting, others were harsh and incoherent.

At some points, Salma felt lost, in the sea of dramatic words; sinking without a life jacket

.

Subject: Re: weekend's rain   *Mon Oct 27 2003*
To: Searcher   *From: The Scribe*

> Yesterday, I did something completely for me; I went on a photo safari. I took almost 100 photos, and I'm hoping a few will be useful for my upcoming artistic endeavors. Since our meeting, many little things have been pushing me to once again create.<

I am so glad you did this. I am so glad you went out and did what you love. I wish I was with you to watch but I am glad you had time to do what you love and do it with peace.

Salma

Subject: Good Morning!   *Tue Oct 28 2003*
To: Searcher   *From: The Scribe*

My Dearest Merrick,

I have so much on my heart to share with you. So much I want and need to say to you.

I awoke this morning at 3:00am and was gripped by joy and sadness. Not happiness Merrick but joy. Joy in the knowledge that I am alive and that you are. Sadness in understanding where you are and where you are coming from and some of what you are going through.

It would surprise you how much God has shown me of your heart. I always find it humbling and breaks me when I look inside pain

I cannot be different than what I am Merrick. God has taught me to love and to be patient and understanding… it is NOT my doing! I cannot push… I can be available… I can be understanding… I can be open… I can be…. but not pushy or demanding.

I happen to love you and if you do not understand that or accept it, there is nothing I can do to make you, except keep loving you.

I see so much in you. So much of what you can be when you are free. Your heart and mind are laden with trouble, your body is suffering from the pains of stress.

God is allowing you a glimpse into what the possibilities are and you run…. it is hard to be loved.

Salma

Subject: Late day!   *Tue Oct 28 2003*
To: Searcher   *From: The Scribe*

Merrick,

I just found out that my day will be a late one again. Actually all this week is a late day… Dr. Shankar is here for his two days of the month... much longer this week.

I do have a break during the day when I will come downtown and give you your phone.

It is a selfish act since I miss your calls in the morning. Hearing you and knowing that you can get in touch with me anytime you want to. I am doing it for me....

Subject: Weekend and misunderstandings.   *Mon Oct 27 2003*
To: The Scribe   *From: Searcher*

Salma,

E-mail is one of my least favorite forms of communication. Many things go unsaid and misunderstood as we saw in the last few e-mails between us. To make it up to you, I would ask that you keep this weekend free so we could go away together and as you suggested several times, talk.

What do you say?

Merrick

Subject: Re: funny fall enthusiasm   *Wed Oct 29 2003*
To: Scribe   *From: Searcher*

My sweetest man,

I often told my daughters that their home was where I am...yes, it is not the place but where your heart is, where your comfort is and where your happiness and peace are at... I truly understand.

It was the context in which you put that note in that e-mail and I was making it clear with you that is all. I know that some of that came from anger of that weekend and how it turned out. I am learning.

I will not allow myself to not tell you how much I want to see you or be with you to spare you pressure. I will tell you

and you can accuse me of pressure if you like…:-)
   I love you always,
   Salma

Subject: Good Morning!   *Fri Oct 31 2003*
To: Searcher   *From: The Scribe*

"The one who wanders independent in the world, free from opinions and viewpoints, does not grasp them and enter into disputations and arguments. As the lotus rises on its stalk unsoiled by the mud and the water, so the wise one speaks of peace and is unstained by the opinions of the world."
   -Mutta Nipata

This morning I embark on something that scares the living daylights out of me. I was asked by one of the companies to change out their amplifier and place the new one in. The new one being only the shell and I have to remove all the components of the old, the boards, the wiring and all the pins to the new amplifier shell…. I am scared to do this but they think that I can…:-)

We shall see what I can do… I am praying that God will hold my hands and keep my mind clear.

BODEGA BAY

This is love: to fly toward a secret sky, to cause a hundred veils to fall each moment. First to let go of life. Finally, to take a step without feet.
                              - Rumi

"I've a surprise for you," said Merrick.

"Another surprise?"

"Yes. D'ya mind?"

"No never. It seems like all the surprises you have for me, are amazing."

They were silent for a few seconds.

"Plus, to tell you the truth, no one has ever given me a surprise, with so many amazing results."

"That's a nice thing to say."

"It is true, too."

Reaching over, he took her hand in his. She loved his hands, big, strong working man, hands. She loved that he was stronger and gentler. He was all she dreamed of in a man and more. Merrick was a gift and she was going to hold it close to her heart, for as long as she was allowed.

She held onto him and he smiled.

"I was rooting through my stuff, you know, my stuff in that room in Toni's house and I found this certificate my mother had given me for my birthday. I called the place, nope not telling," he said, ominously, "and they told me, they would still honor it. I have had this thing for four years and just could not get myself to use it with Toni."

237

"I am sorry Merrick. But I am glad, we could use it. Must be a special place."

"It is," he said, looking shy and secretive. "A surprise. Do you have any plans this weekend?"

"None whatsoever," she said, immediately.

"It's a date then," he said, quietly.

That week went by slowly as Salma, went to her rowing and work. While Merrick, rode the bus into the city to his job. The week went on and on, until the final day, when he called her.

"Alright then," he said, "finally we can go. We will go early. How early can you be ready."

"Very funny," she said, chuckling, "I am up at dawn every morning, come hell or high water. I will be at Moonbeam if you want to pick me up at six."

He, was not amused.

"A little too early for me to be there. I would need to wake up at four to make it. Better yet, I will come and spend the night and we can go together, whenever we both wake up."

Salma was elated. He would spend the night and then they would go together. She loved spending the night with Merrick. It felt like real, everyday, life, when he was there. All life seemed to be suspended, until he was with her.

That night, he arrived in his Honda CRX and parked it beside her car. They were using her car for the trip, packing it with what they would need, for two days and one night.

There was no love making that night. Merrick was tired after the week, and Salma, was only too happy to lie beside him and talk. They built a fire as they sat watching the boat lights on the bay, from her windows. She made two cups of tea, bringing them to the floor, by the fire.

They talked.

"Why did you not use that coupon with Toni?"

"I couldn't do it," he said, sadly. "Every time we went somewhere she hid her drinks; she ended up drunk, and ruined the trip."

Salma was taken aback at the revelation, so easily, divulged.

"It can't be all the time," she tried, evenly.

"You haven't lived with an alcoholic, obviously," he said, seriously. "The last time we went away, I could tell that she was acting squirrley. She swore up and down that she did not have anything to drink, that she did not bring anything with her."

Raising himself on an elbow, his face looked anguished.

"I found it, in her contact lens, wash bottle. I poured it out in the toilet. She demanded to know what I had done with her contact lens cleaner."

He stopped for a moment, to gather his thoughts.

"I remember when we first met," he continued, "we would buy a bottle of wine, and she would drink it and we would get another."

Sighing, he looked for understanding.

"I never thought anything of it, at the time, really. I was drinking with her. But then, came the accidents, and the falling, and the drunken bouts at work."

He looked crushed.

"She accused the pizza boy of attacking her. She called the police and made her accusation. If that poor kid, did not have an alibi of where he was, at the time she claimed, he raped her, he would have been screwed."

Salma was aghast.

"She would hide her bottles everywhere. I found one in the back of the toilet, in the tank. I would find bottles under the sink, in the back, with the cleaning supplies..." he trailed off.

Looking at him, seriously, she had nothing to say.

"I have been to every recovery clinic in the Sonoma, Napa and Marin areas. I am done."

"Not really. You are not done, not really," she said, unexpectedly.

"Don't start that again, please," he begged.

"But it is true, Merrick. You are making her life so hard by being there, all the time. I know that it sounds like I am fishing for myself, and, that I have an ulterior motive, but honestly, you are not allowing her to heal, or move on with her life."

"I know. I know. I have been to enough meetings and Al-Anon meetings to know that. I just don't have the heart to cut her loose and walk away."

"That does not seem kind. It seems cruel to me to allow her to think that you are going to stay. You are using this time to adjust yourself to the idea but she had no idea that you are doing that."

"So now. I am cruel."

Getting up, he paced; then sat on the futon in the living room. She crawled over to him, and sat down at his feet, and looked up in his beautiful, blue, tortured eyes.

"She fell on the coffee table in the house. She was bruised all over. I took her to the emergency room. The police were all over me. They questioned me over and over again. I could tell, they were accusing me of hurting her."

He wiped his face with his hands.

"This nurse came by, a nurse who knew toni well. She stopped and gave the cops hell. She told them to leave me alone. That Toni was a well known alcoholic that this was not new."

"Merrick," said Salma, "I am so sorry."

"You don't know the half of it. I'm trying real hard here to do the right thing."

"Let's not fight," she said, softening. "I am looking forward to this weekend. I cannot imagine allowing Toni, to cause a fight between us."

Standing up, taking her hand in his, as they headed to bed, he kissed her forehead. They lay down, and he held her close to him and they fell asleep.

"No wonder," he whispered. "I cannot imagine that you get into too many fights with guys."

"Not too many, no," she said, drifting off to sleep.

Early the next morning, she woke up and slipped out of bed reaching for her yoga mat. Proceeding with her practice for her twenty minutes, she awakened her muscles and spirit. Praying and stretching, Salma felt happy and solid, on her feet. Her practice helped her stay steady and strong, as she got older.

Merrick had woken up, watched her until she finished, then when she turned, she caught him, looking.

"You could have said, good morning," she laughed, as she came to bed, straddling him.

"You looked great over there and I was being a pig and enjoyed watching you. I like down dog," he said, protecting his chest, while she pummeled him.

He rolled over, taking her with him, off the mattress, and

they stood up, kissing.

"Yuck," she said, wiping her mouth, "morning breath. Let's shower, then maybe, we can brush our teeth."

Showering together was intimate and welcoming. Washing each other, where they could not reach themselves, they touched with familiarity. Washing his hair, for no other reason than, to touch him, she massaged his scalp.

"So, we can stop for coffee first, please?" she begged.

"Sure. What's with this coffee thing, with you?"

"Glad you asked," she rejoined, ready to explain. "Early in the morning, I want to sit down, spend some time quietly, praying and just reading. If I am home, I have a million and one things I need to do, and will get up, and do them. I do not need to do that, so early in the morning. I need to rest, take time, so I can deal with my day. Make sense?" she asked, smartly.

"I get it now. Reasonable. I don't drink caffeine."

"I'm sorry," she said, mockingly.

He smacked her, with the towel as she moved out of the way.

"You do, actually. Every time I get you a mocha, you drink coffee, and apparently, you like it," she added, brazenly.

After getting dressed, they went to Moonbeam for coffee and then headed to, Bodega Bay.

"This town, was made famous by the movie 'The Birds'," Merrick, told her. "You remember that movie?"

"Wow! Yes, I do remember," she cried, enthusiastically. "We went with my grandmother and grandfather, my mom, everyone. It was an open air movie theater, even. It was a scary movie."

"For its time," reasoned Merrick. "It was made, here. It put the town on the map. This small fishing town, that no one had heard of, suddenly, became a tourist attraction, and a resort, of sorts."

Driving along the north coast of Route 1 towards Bodega Bay, Salma was exhilarated, by the beauty of the coast. One of California's most beautiful places she had seen. She loved being here.

Reminding herself that life with Merrick could be a short span, and it could end, she cherished the moments. Or, it could go on, and life would be different. She enjoyed every moment, living it to its fullest.

Arriving, Merrick took her to where the movie, The Birds, by Alfred Hitchcock was filmed. They went to the street where the school teacher, Suzanne Plachette, and the other Scandinavian lady, Tiptin, came running down in terror, in the movie. They stopped by the school building, which was turned into a historical landmark.

"Daphne du Maurier wrote that novella," said Salma. "It was one of her shortest stories."

Sometimes she sounded like a snob, even to herself. Why was there a need to inform him of that tidbit? Did it matter in the scheme of things? Not in the least bit.

Arriving at the Tides' Wharf, Merrick parked and they went inside. The weather was warm and sunny and the seagulls were circling and squawking.

Merrick took her to the counter, where they served seafood asking her if she saw anything she liked. Salma was suddenly, more animated.

"Oh my God," she cried, loudly, "I love crab, Merrick. I have not had good crab in so long. I love crab."

When she arrived at the counter, asking for a whole crab, the man asked if she needed it cleaned. Declining, she confirmed,

"As is, please."

They wrapped her crab in paper. Next, she ordered a pound of cooked shrimp and a slice of peppered, smoked salmon. Asking for two lemons, she requested that, the man behind the counter, cut them for her, in half.

Taking all her loot, the seemingly, ravenous woman, went to one of the tables by the large picture windows, to spread out her feast. Thinking Merrick would share with her, when she was ordering all this, she realized, that he had, no interest.

"I'm not a fan of any of that, stuff," he said, pointing at the spread on the table, as a whole.

"What? You do not like seafood?"

"I like my seafood, a little more, unrealistic," he said, clucking. "What are you going to do with that crab?"

She looked at him, in surprise.

"Eat it," she said, matter of factly, and proceeded to open the paper and set up her food. Laying the paper flat on the table, the famished Salma, poured out the shrimp and the fish. She squeezed lemon on everything.

With total abandon, Salma pulled her sleeves up and started to tear into the crab with both hands. Merrick was riveted in his seat, watching her. This seemed unbelievable to him. Yet, she seemed to know what she wanted, and he was not going to get between her and her crustacean.

Walking up to the counter, Merrick bought a cup of soup for himself.

"What is that?" she asked, incredulously.

"Manhattan clam chowder," he answered, raising an eyebrow.

"Really? You would rather eat that, instead of this incredible food?" she said, with a mouthful of crab.

"Yep," he said, eating gingerly, as he watched her. "I have never seen anyone eat crab, quite, like that."

"How do people eat it?" she asked, seriously.

"In a restaurant with a bib," he said, laughing, "but this, this is much more entertaining and amusing. I love this."

Tearing into the shell of the crab, Salma used her hands and fingers. She used her teeth, for the more stubborn parts. Green goo oozed out, as she opened the back of the crab.

"Mmmmm, mmm, mmmm," she said, as she scooped it up, and put it in her mouth.

Merrick made a disgusted face.

"What was that?" he asked, astounded.

"Green goo. Who knows? The stuff tastes amazing."

A seagull showed up on the other side of the glass, to where Salma was eating. It was making itself crazy watching, trying to break through the barrier between them. It kept pecking at the glass and screeching. Salma would have liked to share with the gull, but it was illegal to feed the critters, and she was not about to ruin her day.

People passed their table, laughing at her spread out feast, her tearing at the crab, with all she's worth.

"Good appetite, your woman," said a man, to Merrick.

Merrick nodded. Placing his elbow on the table, his chin on his palm, he watched her, dumbstruck.

When everything was consumed, she wrapped the scraps in the paper she had spread open, and took it all, to the garbage. There was nothing, recognizable, left of the crab, that Merrick could see, while laughing, as she, licked her chops.

Holding her hands before her, she pushed the women's bathroom door with her back, disappearing into the washroom. She washed as much of the stink off her as she could, then returned, to a still laughing, Merrick.

Leaving the wharf with sated bellies, they walked towards the car. Merrick grabbed her and kissed her mouth.

"You never cease to amaze me," he said, laughing. "There was nothing delicate about that show."

"Delicate? Was I putting on a show?"

"It sure looked like that to me. I'll never forget that, ever. I have to bring you here every year for crab."

Salma realized that Merrick was talking about things he wanted to do with her, in the future. Her day got even better.

Arriving at the Bodega Spa and Inn, Merrick checked them in and driving the car to the general area of their room, parked.

A flag stone set of stairs, took them to their room, which overlooked the ocean. The room, as it were, was a huge suite with white furniture. Glass, floor to ceiling windows at the end, overlooking the water, gave the room a sparkling shine. They both stood looking at their incredible accommodations. When Merrick moved to go further in, the spell was broken and they looked at each other, falling into each other's arms, hysterical.

"Thank your mother, for me," she laughed, holding him. "This is great."

"I was not expecting such a beautiful room, I have to admit. This is a pleasant surprise."

They put their few things away and Merrick asked her to put her bathing suit on.

"I know you like going without clothes, but the hot tubs here are not, for nudists."

They put their bathing suits on and walked out with warm robes, to the hot tub area. The tub was under a white gazebo and surrounded by Plexiglass. You could hear the sound of the ocean which was just a few hundred feet away but you did not get blasted by the cold air that came off the bay. It was a thoughtful design made for luxury and comfort.

The warm water was inviting, and for two hours, they luxuriated in it, after which, they were both relaxed and tired. They returned to the suite, where Merrick started a fire in the fireplace. The warmth of it, sated them. They let it burn, gently, while they showered, getting the chlorine off their skin.

Showering together, of course, Salma basked in touching Merrick. Her thoughts kept going to times when she might not be with Merrick, and a time when she would leave, and never see him again. She tried to stay in the moment, reminding herself, that planning for the future was fruitless. Living in the moment, allowing herself to enjoy her time, was more helpful, and a happier state of mind.

Stepping out of the stall, drying each other with luscious towels from the hotel, the lovers walked to the fireplace, laying down at the hearth, that was warmed by then.

Merrick made love to Salma slowly and leisurely. Combing over her whole body and back again several times, as she allowed him everything she could never allow herself, with anyone else. There was no holding back for him, so, she loved him back for it.

Being too old to romanticize her lovemaking, this proved to be sexy, demanding and romantic. Expecting to wake up from a dream, she did not. Disappear in it, to awaken to its continuing melody.

Laughing several times during their lovemaking, Merrick would look at her surprised. She covered her mouth.

"Sorry. I was having such a good time."

"You shouldn't apologize for enjoying life. I am, too. Your ability to express it, still astonishes me."

"And you have a humble spirit, that does not get its ego bound up in a knot at everything that I do. You, surprise me, too. I am sure someone else, would have thought, that I, was laughing, at him."

"That thought, never occurred to me. By now, I know your laughter. You sound happy. I want to sound like that."

Laying on their sides, facing each other, as the sun started to set, with the fire dying down, Merrick let it, since they were going out to dinner.

"You cannot make anyone happy," she said, suddenly. "Either one is happy, or not. We all get dealt almost the same hand. Troubles find us, all. It depends on how we react."

"Some have it easier than others."

"Really? That sounds like a cop out to me. Everyone gets dealt a hard hand, once in a while. They can either make it work or let themselves sink."

Sitting up straighter, her eyes bored into him.

"As a single Mom, I had so much to deal. The girls were growing up. They were easy to take care of, very good in general. But life has its ups and downs. I remember being on the floor, you know in the hospital, to pick up a patient for a procedure and this nurse looked at me, and said, 'You ever have a bad day, do you? Your life's always perfect and great? Why so happy so early in the morning?'"

Tearing up, as she remembered, she continued, "My male coworker who knew me well, stopped when he heard this, he came up to her face, and said, 'You have no idea what you're talking about. If you can have one day of her life and you can handle it, you have accomplished something'. And he stormed away, taking me with him."

Fondly, remembering that burly, kind, Navy nurse who stood up for her, on more than one occasion, she smiled, wiping her tears away.

"He was a trip. I think his name was Tom. He was gruff, kind and liked me a lot."

Smacking his arm, as he started to be crude, Salma got up.

"Not like that," she said, in mock annoyance. "He was married and very protective. I appreciated his kindness, always."

"Let's go eat," he said. "I'm starving."

After getting dressed, they walked, hand in hand, to the Pluck Restaurant. Merrick's mother had included a generous dinner, for two, in her coupon, allowing them to eat there.

Ushered to a table, that sat at the edge of the cliff, at the water, marveling at the beauty of the scenery. The glass did not obstruct the view of the setting sun.

Ordering was easy, since the menu was limited. Their food arrived. Enjoying the calm, they ate silently.

Heading back to the room, they realized that they were tired. Sleep came within minutes, of laying down on the bed. Holding her closely, as she pushed her back into his arms and body, the two inamoratas, fell soundly asleep.

Deciding not to stay too long the next day, since it was raining, they enjoying the hot tub in the early morning. Then, packed their bags and left.

CIRQUE DU SOLEIL

The ground submits to the sky and suffers whatever comes. Tell me, is the Earth worse for giving in like that ?

- Rumi

Look at Love...
how it tangles
with the one fallen in love .

- Rumi

Subject: this morning's tears   *Thu Nov 13 2003*
To: Scribe   *From: Searcher*

Dearest Salma,

You've told me many times how you "trust" in me. I've done many things these past few days/weeks, moving into two months. My life is rapidly changing to what I need & desire. If nothing else, you've shown me how important it is for me to do this.

As I mentioned in a previous note, the one where your reply was a breathless "OMG"; you are my darling, and if things continue along a trusting path, you will be the partner I've been looking for to spend the second half of my life with.

I do not know any other way than to Love, which is currently causing some troubling difficulties. I realize this more than you're getting. If I'd known you would be in tears this AM, I'd never, ever, have mentioned *my* experience of last night...

Yes, your insecurities around the relationship Toni & I have are valid, real, and will be explained fully on Saturday. The process of this, no matter how it might feel today, will draw you and I closer.

You will enter my world shortly, in an unimaginable way.

Please soothe your emotions, feel alive, work well. My weekend starts in a few hours, yours in a little more than a day. We are doing incredibly well; your fears are hiding the approaching reality, causing too many tears. For now, simply feel the power within this:

Salma, I Love You!

-Merrick

Salma walked in after work, set down her bag, slipped off her shoes and socks by the doorway and stepped softly into her quiet apartment.

Walking through the archway into her bedroom, heading for the bathroom she found her bed tray, set before the windows.

She approached, cautiously.

On the tray were two envelopes, the larger one, on the bottom.

A note was set on top.

She smiled. Merrick had been here. She smiled again.

She reached for the envelope with anticipation and excitement.

My Treasured One,
Welcome to my world.
Enclosed, you will find the following:
#1 Note - these initial instructions.
#2 Small Envelope
#3 Large Envelope - Open ONLY after beginning your journey.

This small envelope contains money, in many denominations for your careful use, and a pen. This money (and only this money) will be used for your Saturday transportation & comfort. You will not use your car, thus have no access to the "stuff" inside it all weekend.

What I want you to do is plan on being at your SF destination by 3:30 PM on Saturday. From the moment you walk out your door beginning your journey, I want you to account for every cent along the way, knowing I can be a kind & generous soul. I *expect* you to be as well... The choice you have to make is this: how much of the money should be left over?? Circumstances you encounter will determine any "right" answer.

When you arrive in SF, I want you to feel *alive", refreshed, and not travel weary. Personal energy conservation can be a good thing. The least expensive path will be to walk to the Sausalito Ferry Terminal, and from there, a -long- hike to your destination. If it's raining, you'll be quite wet... not good!

The most expensive way to get to your destination will be to take a taxi all the way from your apartment. If it's raining, you'll be dry, but will have used a great deal of your money…

I'll help you out with this first decision, by suggesting you open the large envelope once aboard the Ferry to SF…:-))

Your actual experience may vary.

The last possible boat you can catch leaves for SF at 1:45 PM boat. See schedule for details. Take an earlier boat if you wish, but DO NOT miss this last possible boat. If you do, you'll have to take a taxi all the way.

This ferry should arrive in SF around 2:15 PM. This should give you plenty of time to continue your journey into my world. Once on the SF side, either walk, take a cab, or make your way using some combination of BART / Muni.

All My Love,

-Merrick

PS, don't be surprised if it feels like you're being watched.

Restlessly, Salma walked around her small apartment wondering what was going to happen the next day. Surprises were not part of her life, until Merrick. Her mind was racing.

Who could she call to ask for assistance in doing this? Picking up the phone, she called her friend, Melvin, for help.

Salma was in anticipation all next morning. Of course, she wanted to know what was in that large envelope, but she would not open it, it was a matter of trust and from the looks of it, he trusted her. So, she waited.

Melvin came to pick her up at eight am. Deciding on Cafe Toronto, on Bridgeway, for a cup of tea and a chat, Melvin drove them there.

"So what is this all about??"

"You know," she started, "I met this man on line, the one you met when you came to dinner that night, and …."

Explaining what had transpired so far, then explaining what was about to happen, she realized, that it all sounded crazy, truly unstable.

"You've got to be kidding," he responded to her story, incredulously. "So let me get this straight; you have no idea what he has planned for you and you are still going, to meet him!"

"Yes," she nodded, smiling, "I am."

"What if it's something you don't want to do, or even like to do?"

"Ahhhh, I see where this is going. I am not sure that you have ever had anyone care for you, so much, that what you decide to do, is a moot point."

Awaiting some recognition from him, she realized that none was forthcoming. He looked at her, blankly.

"What we do, or where we go, is not what matters. It is just being with him, and around him, that matters the most."

"That is absolutely incredible," he said, shaking his head. "You are probably right, I have never had anyone that liked me that much."

Looking at him, she noticed, how handsome he was. She noticed how he smiled and it warmed her heart.

"You should introduce me again, sometime," he told her.

"I will."

"How does a man get a woman to do that for him?"

"Easy. Pay attention. Take the time. Find the right woman."

"I seem to always find the wrong one."

"One too young, maybe? It depends. We have known each other since I moved here. You never asked me out."

Embarrassed, he changed the subject.

"It's time to leave. You will miss the ferry."

Getting up, they headed to the Sausalito ferry. She bought her ticket with the money Merrick gave her, as instructed. Melvin stayed with her until she got on.

He kissed her cheek and said, "Let me know how it goes and if I do not hear from you, I will call to make sure that you are, really, alright."

"Don't call. I will probably not answer my phone this weekend," she answered back, waving, as she walked away, "and if I die this weekend, then I have lived, and am happy to go, quietly."

"That is not funny and I am not kidding," he shouted.

Stopping on the dock, She turned around, covering her eyes with her hand from the sun, "Neither am I."

Getting on the ferry with her bag and envelope, sitting where she could see the Golden Gate Bridge as they crossed the bay, she watched as the water and the sky passed by, slowly. The ferry was slower on the weekends, and she was lazily watching in anticipation.

Pulling out the sheets of paper, placed in the large envelope, Salma was intrigued.

She found a note from Merrick.

#3 Large Envelope

Hopefully you've opened this as you've settled into your seat on the Ferry. You're feeling on time, and life has an "interesting" feel.

Yes, I slipped a few times, giving away the truth. You *are* going to see the Cirque Du Soleil performance of Alegria at 4 PM. Your ticket is inside the small envelope I've attached to this note. When you get there, you'll see many tents. They open at 3:30 PM, which is when I want you to walk in & find your seat...

Hopefully you've used your funds wisely making yourself comfortable along the way. Less than great "food" & water will be available as you pass through the show tents. However, there's no need to buy any "merchandise"...

I'll be joining you as the show begins.

overnight bag
clothes, shampoo, conditioner, vitamins, pills, water, wallet, brush,
room - jacuzzi, view east (sunrise) / west (to ocean horizon), beds, food, flowers,
ice chest, glasses, plates, napkins,
4 lengths of 3/8" braided nylon

Flipping through the packet, she found a ticket to a circus. She had no idea what Cirque Du Soleil was, or ever even, heard of it.

In awe, she looked at the brochure. She never thought she would enjoy these kinds of performances. Refusing to enjoy other people's misery, and the use of animals in unnatural ways, she had never gone to a circus. She refused to be entertained by other people's danger .

A bleeding heart or a wing nut liberal, she was not, but she had never even, taken her daughters to a circus.

Interesting. Melvin was right, in a way. She heard him.

'What if you do not even like where you are going?'

Leaning back, she closed her eyes. In a few minutes, she would be in San Francisco, and the mystery would be solved.

San Francisco never seemed to lose its charm and beauty, as she came off the ferry, to the dock. Walking to The Embarcadero street, she hailed a cab.

Explaining to the cab driver where she needed to go, he started driving, as she settled in her seat.

As she arrived, she noted, that these were white circus tents. They filled the ball park, parking lot. No red and white, hmmm.

 Dragging her overnight bag, she sat at the very front, in her assigned seat, turning around, to people watch. Looking at the crowds and the children, wide eyed and happy, she tried to relax.

She knew that Merrick would arrive soon, and was looking forward, to seeing him. About 4:30, he showed up by her seat; with another woman.

"Salma, this is Toni. Toni this is Salma."

Waiting for the women to say something, Merrick stood, looking, from one to the other. The two rivals, said hello tightly, and he sat down, between them. Salma was on his right and Toni was on the left.

Not sure how to react or what she should do, Salma leaned away from Merrick. Should she just stand up, leave right that minute, and go. Should she sulk, make a scene? She leaned further away from Merrick. He leaned closer to her, whispering, in her ear.

"You kept telling me you wanted to meet. I found the best way for you two, to meet."

"Or," she said, irked, "you could have warned both of us, and we could have had dinner somewhere. Springing it on us like this, is probably not cool; with her, either. She does not seem, comfortable," she hesitated, at a loss for words.

"Neither do you."

"I am getting there," she answered, shortly. "Just a bit of a surprise."

The two older women, did not talk at all for the first part of the show. Toni never caught her eye and it was easily done, since they were sitting side by side, making it, unlikely, to look at each other. Merrick was seated between them, so conversation, if there was to be any, had to be, over him.

The show was amazing. Since Salma had never seen one of those before, she was fascinated, loving it.

During the intermission, Merrick stood up to stretch his legs.

"Would you like something from the bar, outside?"

"No, thanks," said Salma.

"No," said Toni, shaking her head.

"Alright, I am going to go to the bathroom, before they start up again."

He walked out leaving the x-wife, and the girlfriend alone; to themselves.

"Quite a surprise," said Salma, making conversation. "It is good to finally meet you."

"Yes, it is. I've been asking Merrick to meet you for the past two months."

"Same here," said Salma. "It is awkward, but not terrible."

"I thought I'd be spending the weekend with Merrick, by myself," said Toni, sounding resentful.

"Yes, I am sorry. I did too," said Salma, abashed.

Realizing that the conversation, was not going well, as she was hoping it would go, Salma, looked down at her program. Pretending to find it very interesting, she tried to ignore the obvious hostility.

Thankfully, Merrick returned. The two women did not have to speak anymore.

When the show started up again, Salma was caught up in the magic and beauty of the performers and the music.

When the show ended, they stood up, and started to walk out of the tent, to the parking lot.

"We brought the van," said Merrick. "I thought that it would be easy and lots of room for everyone."

He smiled at both women and they smiled back.

By that time, Salma, had reconciled herself to meeting Toni, while having a good time. It did not look like Toni, was having a good time, at all.

Unlocking the van, Merrick put Salma's bag in the back. He opened the door for her, as she got in. Then, he got in the driver's seat.

"From here, we have reservations at the Lodge, in Tiburon," he explained. "You two kept telling me that you would like to meet. So, I arranged it for you, to spend time together."

"Sounds fine," said Salma.

Toni did not say anything.

Salma was not and never considered herself a beauty but Toni angry, was even less than that. Her anger made her even more unattractive.

Driving across the Golden Gate Bridge, Merrick headed into the peninsula of Tiburon. They arrived without incident at the lodge, and he walked inside to confirm their reservations.

"You know," said Toni, turning around, in her seat," you're not the first or last woman that he's going to be with."

"I am sure," said Salma, caught unawares.

"You're not his first fling, nor his last."

"I am sure," said Salma, again.

"Did he tell you that he lives with me?"

"Yes, he did," replied Salma, with more command of her faculties.

"What did you think of that?"

"What do you mean?" Salma asked, impertinently.

"We are still living as husband and wife."

"You mean you sleep together? Yes, I know. He told me."

Salma knew that she was not being kind to this woman. She baited her.

"You find that alright?" asked Toni, again.

"Strange, not alright. Just what it is. You are divorced."

"Divorced, but living and sleeping together," said Toni, angrily.

"That to me, means, that you have allowed him to move back in, and you sleep with him."

"You are stealing my husband."

"X-husband. I am not stealing, your, husband," said Salma emphasizing the word, husband.

"Yes, you are doing some stealing. He does live with me."

"Stealing implies ownership. You gave up that right. But,

that is not an issue, anyway."

"He'll come back to me, you know. He always does," she retorted, bitterly.

"Great," said Salma, suddenly relieved. "Great, then you have nothing to worry about. When he is done with me, you can have him back."

There were a few minutes of silence, when Toni said,

"This time," she said, tentatively, "I am worried. You're not the same, like the others."

Before she had time to explain, Merrick was back ushering them to the suite, that he had rented for them, for the night.

They walked into an incredible room, with one large bed, a raised hot tub and a wonderful shower with eight heads and sliding doors. They walked in, awestruck.

Purple flowers in four baskets, three bouquets in vases scattered all around the room, adorning the corners, greeted them.

"This is beautiful," said Salma.

"Yes, it is," said Toni.

Both women walked in, and set their bags down.

"I am getting in the water," said Salma, immediately, as she started to take her clothes off, while wrapping herself in a wonderfully, lush towel.

She walked up four steps then walked down the two steps into the hot tub. The hot water enveloped her, and she sighed.

Merrick and Toni were arguing. She seemed angry, and their whispering was loud enough, for Salma to hear.

"Whatever it is you and her are planning, I'm not gonna to be involved in."

"What're you talking about?" asked, an angry, Merrick.

"You don't think that I am having sex with the two of you,

I hope? That's not what you were thinking, is it?" she spat out, infuriated.

"I thought nothing of the sort. I wanted to spend the weekend with Salma, but didn't want to leave you behind, so, I brought you with me. Did I do the wrong thing, Toni?"

"I thought we're going to spend a whole weekend together, alone," she complained.

"No we're not. I was taking Salma to the Cirque and had it planned months ago. I decided not to leave you behind. She seems to be fine with it," he said, looking over at Salma, in the water.

"She seems to be fine with everything," said Toni, indignantly.

Merrick walked away in a huff, as he took his clothes off. He stepped into the water with Salma. They stayed away from each other, out of respect, for Toni and talked quietly, about the show.

"The flowers are beautiful," said Salma. "I love the purple Merrick. They are gorgeous."

"I ordered 'em and the woman on the phone, asked me, if I was getting married. I told her, that today, was the first day of my new life."

Merrick sounded, tearful.

Toni came out of the bathroom with a towel around her, then, she slipped into the hot tub. She seemed less angry, but certainly reserved.

"I guess it was time for us to meet," she said, pursing her lips tightly.

"Yes," smiled Salma, "it was time. I have been asking. I would have preferred some advance notice," she continued, looking at Merrick, sharply, "but, this is turning out, to be fine."

"Yes, I would've liked some notice too."

Within a few minutes, Toni stood, and walked up the steps.

"I think that I'll go to bed. I'm very sleepy."

She dried herself off and slipped under the covers, leaving Merrick and Salma, in the water.

"This is very awkward," sang Salma, in a hushed voice; putting a sing song on, the word, awkward.

"Yes, it is," said Merrick. "You're doing fine."

"It seems cruel, though."

"No, it is not. She knows that I am seeing you and she has been asking me for months, to meet you."

"That was just talk Merrick, to show you how open she is, to whatever you want to do."

He sighed.

"I guess it backfired, since I believed her, and here we are," he said, with a flourish of his hands.

Sliding over to his side, she hugged him, kissing his mouth, quietly.

He pushed her away, firmly, but gently.

"Let's not make things worse," he quipped.

She giggled, quietly, and moved away, but not before grabbing him for a second.

The night was long and quiet. Toni had started to snore the moment her head hit the pillow.

"Alcohol," he answered, the unasked question.

"What alcohol?"

"Who knows where!" he exclaimed, disgusted.

When Merrick and Salma got in bed, he had one woman on either side of him. Within the hour, they fell in fitful sleep.

As usual, Salma, woke up early. Trying to sneak out of

bed, Merrick caught her arm.

"I am going to shower," she said, mouthing the words, silently.

"I will come with you," he responded.

The shower was amazing; expansive really. They turned all the shower heads on, and were pelted from all angles, loving every moment. Showering together, was one of the things they cherished.

A knock on the bathroom door, brought Merrick to open it. Toni was up. They exchanged a few harsh words and he came back, looking exasperated.

"She is not happy."

"No kidding," said Salma, laughing. "I would not have been happy either."

They dried each other off.

Walking out to the room, to where Toni was getting her belongings ready, for a shower, Salma respectfully, stayed out of her way.

Merrick went back in the bathroom for something, leaving Salma and Toni, alone again.

"I would have liked to shower with him," she said, indignantly. "I never get to shower with him."

"I am sorry," said Salma, genuinely. "You should be able to. I love to shower with him."

Toni picked up her towel, and stormed into the bathroom.

Merrick came out and sat down on one of the armchairs.

"This is going to be a long weekend," commented, Salma.

"Yes it's looking that way, huh?" he responded. "I asked if she wanted to go home. We brought the van, so she could leave, if she wanted to. I offered several times and she refused."

Salma let a few seconds pass, then, she brought it up.

"She told me that she would like to shower with you. You do not shower with her?"

Merrick looked up amazed then shook his head, in resignation.

"She had me, forever. She never comes in the shower when we're together, ever. I have been with that woman for twenty years, Salma, she has never entered my shower."

Salma stared, in surprise.

"Yeah," he said, "I told'er that we could get a cab, get your car, in a heartbeat. She refused. She wants to spend the rest of the weekend doing whatever I'd planned for us."

"I am glad, I guess. She does not look happy, at all."

"No, she's quite angry. But, she's coping."

All three spent a few minutes, packing. No one talked. Salma smiled several times, at Toni.

Ready to leave within a few minutes, Merrick put the bags in the van and got in the driver's side.

"Anyone leave anything or need anything before we go on with our adventure? I've got to settle the bill."

Both women shook their heads.

Merrick got out, and they were alone, again.

"You scare me," said Toni. "You are not the same, like the others, and that bothers me."

She turned in her seat to look at Salma.

"I am here for only six months, Toni. I am leaving in six months, and you can have him back."

"He may not come back this time. You're different. You bother me."

"I am sorry."

"No you're not. You're not sorry at all. You looked like you were gonna make love to my husband in front of me last night."

"X husband," said Salma, nastily. "X husband. You two, are divorced. You keep saying that, and I keep having to remind you. Do not accuse me of things that have not happened."

Merrick came back and both women stopped talking.

"Okay, everyone alright?" said, the oblivious man.

He looked at both women, then turned to the wheel. He started the car, driving out of the parking lot, to the city.

"We're going to the Asian Museum. Have you been to the Asian Museum, Salma?" he asked, breaking the silence.

"No, I have not been before."

"It's special and there's a special exhibition this weekend that'll end soon."

The drive was not long, and all was quiet, until,

"I was thinking," said Merrick, suddenly, "we should do something together, for Thanksgiving. Would you ladies like to do that?"

"Yes, I would love to," said Salma, immediately.

Toni's body, stiffened. Then she tried to relax, saying quietly, "I suppose that would be fine. Yes, I would not mind that."

"Where do you want to go?" asked Salma, stimulated by the thought, of spending more time with Merrick.

"I was thinking that we should got to Yosemite. Have you been, Salma?"

"Once again," she said, sounding gratified, "I have not been to Yosemite. I love this. So much to see and I have not seen it before."

The Asian Museum of Art was beautiful. Walking through it, they saw statues, paintings and best of all, for Salma, were the hand made Kimonos, on display.

After the museum, everyone was hungry. Merrick took them to Fort Mason, to a vegetarian restaurant overlooking the bay. The food was good, and they ate, with relish.

That Sunday continued without incident. Merrick and Toni dropped Salma off, at her apartment, around seven in the evening.

Merrick got out of the car and came around to open her door, holding her tightly.

"I will miss you, tonight."

"So will I," she said, kissing him. "Come back soon."

YOSEMITE

Now I am sober and there's only the hangover and the memory of love .

- Rumi

Thanksgiving came around. It was time to go off on their new adventure; Merrick, Salma and Toni. Salma thought about this, many times. She wanted to reassure herself, that things were normal but, she knew, they were not. She was going away with the man she loved, and his x-wife. Nothing about that, was normal.

The other solution to this dilemma, was to stay home, let him go away, with Toni, alone. Which meant, that she does not spend any time with him, and he would remain miserable.

When they had discussed this, Merrick explained that he was having a very hard time leaving Toni behind, in any - way.

"I've lived with this woman for twenty years," he tried to explain to, Salma. "I loved her so much when we were together, and our life was good. The only problem we ran into, was her drinking."

"That is a big problem," said Salma. "You cannot solve her problem, yourself."

On the other hand, Salma knew that she could not cut off this woman, forever, from the man she claimed to love; away, from his life. It will take time, knowing she had lots of it.

The issue here was, how much time does she want to

269

spend, away from Merrick? And, even more pressing, how much would she tolerate, in order to spend, most of her time, with him?

'This was not a difficult decision,' she thought, to herself. 'I can do this. After all, Toni is just a human being in trouble, in pain. I can handle people in trouble and kindness will not kill me.'

A prig, she sounded like a prig, even to herself. She was analyzing too much, instead of handling this with grace, she was acting like she was doing someone, a favor. Either do it or do not do it, without all the, soap box, nonsense, she told herself, sternly.

Deciding to go, the subject was closed for her. The consequences, the ways to do it and all that, would come as the days went by, along with the time they spend, together.

Merrick and Toni came to pick her up in the van, again. Merrick put her bag in the back. Toni sat up front, with him, again, noted by Salma, to herself. She gritted her teeth then reminded herself, that she decided to do this, and to stop, acting like a child.

As soon as she decided this, she started having a good time; letting it all go, hanging out, for a fun ride.

The trip to Yosemite was uneventful, but beautiful. Salma had never been to this stretch of California, which left her marveling at the beauty and grandeur, of it all.

"This is so beautiful," she said, in wonderment. "I am so amazed, that there is so much beauty, yet to see. I used to think that there was nothing more beautiful than the East Coast, but this is amazing."

"What is so beautiful about the East Coast," said Merrick, sarcastically.

"You have not been to Lake George or the Adirondak

Mountains, if you ask, that," she retorted. "Don't you be, dissing, New York," she continued, saucily.

"I understand you've got kids?" asked Toni, out of the blue.

"Yes. I have two grown daughters. Hardly kids."

"Do you see them, often?"

"No, we see each other, maybe, once a year," mused Salma. "Everyone is busy with their own life, and forging forward," she laughed, feeling edgy and adventurous.

"We never had children," said Toni, suddenly, again.

"Yes. I thought you guys agreed that you did not want children."

"Agreed, yes," said Toni, hesitantly.

They both looked at Merrick, who seemed to grasp the wheel tightly, not looking at either one, nor taking his eyes off the road. He, obviously, was listening.

"I taught school all my life, and did not think that I wanted children," she continued, softly.

"Yes, that would do it," said Salma, keeping up.

They were silent for a few minutes.

"How long have you been single?" asked Toni.

"Long enough," said Salma, laughing. "Long enough to not want to be single, any longer. It was fun though, while it lasted."

Thinking for a moment, Salma said, "I would say about five years, on and off, with different guys. Really great men, kind and smart."

"Why didn't you hook up with any of 'em?"

"No long term interest, on either part. It was always something. They wanted children, mine were grown. I do not want any children. They had small children, living with them, most of the time."

271

She laughed out, loudly.

"I did not fit the bill in the looks department. Some were too old, some were much too young. I have grey eyes, they want brown. I like physically strong men, while they were small and wimpy."

She laughed again, making Merrick, laugh with her.

"Yes, I'm a strong man. Zugzug!" he mocked.

"Stronger than I am," she replied.

California byways were beautiful. Then, arriving at Curry Village, in Yosemite Valley, Merrick parked. He pointed out the tent structures, that looked like, square yurts.

"We are staying here tonight. Since it's Thanksgiving, reservations were hard to come by. We stay in the Ahwahnee Hotel, the next two nights, though."

Not knowing the difference, this could not dampen Salma's enthusiasm for this arrangement. They got into their tent, which had a large bed, in the middle of the room. There was a television set, at the foot of the bed, and pretty much, nothing else.

Putting down their bags, Salma noticed that Toni had two, while Merrick, had his own bag, much larger than Salma's.

"Do you have everything you need in here?" he asked, making fun of her sack.

"Yes. I am used to traveling for work, usually very light. I change the look of my clothes with a shawl or a scarf, you know," she demurred.

Realizing that she was doing it again, Salma stopped herself. Again with the catty, poor behavior. This relationship has been showing her, some of her serious flaws.

"I need my hair dryer, wherever I go," said Toni, sourly. "My hair does whatever it feels like, and I've got to tame it."

"Your hair looks like mine. You have curly hair, right? "

"Yes, I do."

"Then let it go, after you wash it. It will do whatever it feels like, and you will not have to worry about it."

"Some of us, have to worry more than others."

"But you do not have to. Your hair is beautiful."

"My mother told me, that I look like a frog. Believe me, I have to care about my hair."

Salma walked out of the tent, to look around, leaving Toni and Merrick inside, to talk. She heard murmuring and intense whispering; but she decided, she did not want to hear what was being said, so, she walked, to explore around the tent area.

The tents were close to each other. A metal, lock box, sat outside each of the structures, for anything resembling food. There were 'Beware of Bear' signs, everywhere. She learned this, when she saw other people, putting their food stuffs, in there. While a father explained to his children, why he was using that box.

"Yes," he said, "Mommy has to put her makeup in there also, or else the good smell of all those things she uses, will attract the bears, and they will come in and help themsel....."

They walked away and she could not hear more of what he said. She smiled, at how the children were wide eyed with wonder, at his stories. She thought of what she brought with her, and deciding that she should go back, put some of her makeup, meager as it was, into the lock box, she walked back.

She stepped into the tent and found Merrick and Toni facing off, and both, looked angry.

"Sorry," she said, as she stood there, unsure of her next move. "I have some makeup in my bag, ... ummmm...., thought maybe, I should put it in the lock box."

"Yes, that'd be a good idea," said Merrick, trying to smile.

Walking to her bag, she took out the small pouch, then started for, the door.

"It is a beautiful day outside," she said, pointlessly. "You guys coming out?"

"We are coming out, to play, soon," said Toni, sarcastically.

Salma walked out, plopping down on the stoop, waiting for the irate couple, to finish their conversation. She was sure she was the reason for the conflict, but was not sure, how, she could fix it.

"No," she heard, Merrick, say, "No. I was going to bring *her*, Toni. I didn't want to leave *you* at home, to have Thanksgiving, alone. I wanted this with *her*. *She* agreed, to have *you*, come along. Do you understand this Toni? *She* was gracious and agreed. *You*, were not, coming," he emphasized, the last few words.

"I am not going to be humiliated by your nonsense, anymore," Toni said, enraged.

"I told you what we were doing. Would you like to go home?"

"I'll take the van. It's mine," she said, petulantly.

"Yes, I know. You can take the van."

Salma could hear her voice, relenting, suddenly.

"I wanted to spend Thanksgiving alone, with you," she heard Toni say, softly, unhappily.

"I want to spend it with Salma, and could not leave you behind," he said, softening his voice.

"Why does she have to be here?" said Toni, whining.

"I am not doing this anymore. I am leaving now. If you

want to come, get your stuff."

She could hear scuffling, and the door opened, finding him standing, above her, in the sunlight.

"Hey," she said, quietly. "I am sorry."

"No need," he said, looking down at her. "She knew."

He put his finger to his lips, she did not say much more.

Toni was ready and came out. They spent the day hopping from one bus to the other, visiting all the villages, in Yosemite Valley. They visited the waterfalls, which were nothing but a trickle, since it was Autumn.

"The best time to see the falls is in the Spring," he said, with anticipation. "Maybe, we can come in the Spring?"

They ate at the Curry Village, cafeteria, enjoying all the amenities and beauty of the valley.

Their conversations went better. Toni started to talk to Salma; they started talking, without anger. Salma was kind and Toni was guarded.

Having the upper hand in this situation, Salma did not want to drive, her advantage. She tried to be quiet, attentively listening to Toni. She realized that this was a bright, intelligent and very pleasant, woman.

But, she had never seen her drink, and that, she would rather not see. She kept the conversation light and easy and answered any questions Toni put to her.

That first night they sat up in bed, watching, Finding Nemo, since Salma had not seen it, and had mentioned that to Merrick, a few weeks earlier. He thought of it, of course, and brought the movie for her to see.

They slept in the bed with Merrick in the middle. Nothing inappropriate happened in that bed and the night was spent, quietly. Toni fell asleep very quickly, while Merrick and Salma, talked softly, until they drifted off, to sleep.

The next morning, they had breakfast at the cafe again. Merrick had pancakes, Salma had eggs, bacon and cheese while Toni ate fruit and pastry. When he went to the bathroom, they were alone, again.

"I wanted children," said Toni, unexpectedly. "I wanted children, so badly."

"I thought you did not want children," said Salma, sincerely.

"He didn't want children, not me."

"He changed his mind?"

"What?" asked Toni, surprised. "What d'ya mean?"

"I mean after you got married, he changed his mind?"

"No. No, he never, wanted children."

"So, you knew before you married him, that he did not want children."

Toni looked at her and the old hostility, returned.

"I know what you're doing. You think, you're very clever."

"I am not sure what you are talking about. I was clarifying what you were saying to me," said Salma, guarded.

Then she caught on. She had cornered her in an illusion, a lie and she felt assaulted. Not intentionally. Or was it intentional? Was Salma playing low and dirty, with this delusional, woman?

Who was this person who behaved so abominably? Salma could hardly recognize herself when she behaved so poorly.

"You are so smart," said Toni. "You think I don't know what you're doing?"

"Toni, I am sorry, really. I was not trying to do anything…."

Merrick arrived at the table and the conversation stopped.

He could tell that something was up, but did not engage.

They hopped on the bus and returned to the tent.

Packing their stuff, heading to the Ahwahnee Hotel, they rode in the van, that belonged to Toni.

The Ahwahnee Hotel, as they approached its walls, was an incredible building, set in the middle of all the grey granite mountains. It was built to blend in, with its surroundings. The walls were high and not decorative, just simple, standing straight up.

Salma beamed.

The luggage was picked up by the bell boy, whom they followed, to the reception desk.

Inside, was warmed by so many fireplaces. They were huge and all lit up. The wood chunks were large, glowing, even in the daylight.

Salma wandered away, as Merrick checked them in.

Set around the fireplaces, beautiful, full, couches and chairs, were amazingly, luxurious; made for comfort and lingering. It was a scene out of a Dickens book, and she, fell in love with the architecture and the furniture.

Merrick came to find her, and all three of them, walked out the back by the swimming pool, and down the walkway. They meandered towards the cabins, set in the back, of the huge structure.

"All I could find, last minute, was this cabin," he said, conspiratorially.

When the bell boy opened the door to the cabin, Salma, inhaled loudly. She was ecstatic. The 'cabin' as they called it, was a charming cottage, with two huge beds in the middle, with windows, surrounding it all. A large fireplace took up a whole wall, by the door.

Venturing further in, she came upon the large bathroom,

with lush towels, a big shower head, and two sinks. She turned around to walk out, as Toni passed her, to use the bathroom.

Merrick tipped the young man, closing the door behind his retreating form. And as Salma turned, he went over and hugged her.

"Thank you so much, Merrick. This is so beautiful. It is amazing, really. Cabin, my butt, this is so, so grand. An English cottage, if I ever saw one," she pattered on, as she, hugged him back.

He put her away from him, gently, laughing in her eyes.

"You look, so, happy."

"I am. I am, so very much. I am sorry, you are not."

"I am. I just have to be kind."

"Yes, to your detriment."

He nodded.

"This is not good for either of you," she said, logically. "She is miserable, and so are you. I am the only one, who is not," she said, flopping on the bed.

When he sat beside her, she sat up, leaning into him. He looked at her, then stood up, pulled her up. He started moving the beds together.

"We are not having, this," he said, determined, "we are not having, sharing wars."

By the time Toni came out of the bathroom, Merrick had both beds together, and the quilts covered all, making it into one big, huge bed.

Salma helped, sniggering, being silly, all the way, always getting in his way, as many times as she could, until, he shoved her, playfully.

"That should make the staff raise an eyebrow or two," he said, perversely.

"Sure will," responded Salma, with a twinkle in her eye.

"Like I said," repeated Toni, coming out of the bathroom, looking around her, "whatever it is you two have planned, I am not part of this," she made circular motions, at the bed, with her right pointer. "Whatever, you are doing with the beds."

"Not planning, anything," said Merrick, "but sleep."

"I really need to spend some time with you, alone," started Toni. "We should, maybe, split the day. We go off alone, for a few hours and then you come back, then you can go out with Salma."

For a few seconds, there was silence. Salma broke the spell.

"Yes, we could do that. You guys can go, do whatever you want to do, for a while. I could use the time to read and chill, actually."

Merrick looked angry, but resigned.

He snatched his wallet, pushed it in his back pocket and Toni, following him, they walked out the door.

The main lobby was inviting, with its fireplaces and large couches, where Salma went with her book. She opened and closed the pages several times, trying to concentrate, which seemed futile.

Two hours later, Merrick showed up, as she was turning down an invitation, from a young man, who sat beside her. The object of her affection, sat on the couch beside her. Taking his hand, she looked at him, searchingly.

"Who's that?" he demanded.

She shrugged.

"Not sure."

"What did he want?"

Laughing at his insecurity, Salma spoke, seductively, "Some adorable guy who wanted to take me into the woods and ravish me…"

She leaned away from Merrick, as smirking, he caught her, close to him.

"Your turn," he said, sounding exasperated. "Where would you like to go?"

"I do not need a *turn*, " she said, emphatically. "Let's go find her, go to lunch, or whatever you want to do. I am not playing this game. Time to grow up."

She stood, like greased lightning, pulling him up with her. Walking hand in hand to their rental, they entered the cabin, to find Toni sitting, on one of the armchairs, looking, miserable and dejected.

"Hey," said Salma, "We are back. Thanks for the time alone. Let's go eat."

Toni looked up at her. There were unshed tears in her eyes. Salma realized, that this woman, was trying to hate her. She was struggling not to enjoy her company. Salma felt sad for her. Walking up to Toni, she pulled her up, putting the crook of her elbow, around her neck.

"Come on, let's go. You can hate me, later."

Toni laughed, a short brittle laugh, but she put her arm around Salma's waist. They walked out the door, together, into the cold, with Merrick following, quietly.

Dinner time came, and Merrick made reservations in the lodge dining room. The two women dressed, beautifully. Salma was in a Chanel taupe, black polka dotted dress, with a taupe shawl and black heels and black, silk stockings. While Toni, wore a black princess dress with sandals and a silk jacket. Both women looked coifed and primped.

Merrick wore a blue shirt and black pants. The blue in the shirt, picked up the color of his eyes, which radiated with excitement, for the first time, in days. Everyone, seemed relaxed and comfortable, finally.

They arrived at the dining room, reservation desk. Merrick had both hands full, with the hands of both women, one in each. The Maitre'D pointedly, looked at his hands, from left to right, and back again.

"Reservations under Merrick, for three," said the Don Juan, smiling.

The Maitre'D smiled, knowingly, almost winked, but decorum won over his impulse. He led them to a table, right before him. Merrick and Salma exchanged glances. The man was putting them right before him, so he could observe, the exchange.

Within a few minutes, the whole dining room staff, seemed to buzz with the news. A man, arrived, holding hands with two women, who were, relatively attractive.

Many of the male workers, waiters, bus boys, even Sous Chefs passed their table, nodded at Merrick, seeming to enjoy and in, on the joke. Even the piano player, knew, and would look over and smile at Merrick, playing "Anything Goes".

The fact that these two women were in their late 40s, made not a difference, to anyone. They were the talk of the dining room. They were, the sweethearts of the place. Their daring, was an adventure.

The three intrepid souls, talking, laughing, while they ate. Nothing was ruining this evening, it seemed. Toni was relaxed and content, suddenly. She was not angry or venomous. She reached over several times to touch Merrick's sleeve or his hand. He tenderly, touched her back.

The crowning glory was when the Chef himself came out of the kitchen, walked around the perimeter of the dining hall and looked over at Merrick and nodded, in approval, commending his courage, in doing what they all wished, they could do.

Dinner was a hit, in all aspects. Amazing food, whether to look at, or to taste. The music, was languid. The lighting, was soft. The attention, was delightful.

The time in Yosemite showed Merrick things he needed to see. The time in Yosemite explained things Salma needed to understand. The time in Yosemite showed Toni where it all ended, where she needed to start a new life, without Merrick.

The drive home was silent but content, and sad. Everyone made decisions in their own head, about what they were to do with their lives. It was a successful journey, for all.

NO HOLDS BARRED

Don't grieve. Anything you lose comes round in another form."

- Rumi

It was not that life could not be lived, without him; it is more that, she did not want, to live life, without him. One could go without food or drink for a while, and then, there is a dire need to remain healthy, when hunger kicks in. It felt like that, being with him. She could be without him, but then a dire need would well up, inside her, then she would want, to be with him, around him.

He awoke in her, feelings of warmth and love. He was loving and caring. When she came close, she felt literal heat and she felt heat of passion, arise in her.

He had not spoken the words; or told her that he loved her, because he was not aware that he did. He showed her, which was much more what she needed and desired. Words came and went, but actions, spoke louder, and much clearer. He could write those words, but never spoke them, out loud.

In years past, in her teens and twenties she learned a very hard lesson, that often escaped, most of her women friends. Those were the same women, who called her cold and 'like a man'. She learned, that assumption, was a set up for disappointment, in relationships.

A little attention made some women, assume, that they were living the rest of their life, with that particular man. Ever after as it were, like Cinderella did, and procreate, as God intended for them.

If a man asked a girl, to save the seat next to her, for him, at a concert, then he was the one, he was the father of her children; the man on the white horse, who would spirit her away, to the life of luxury, barf!

Yet, she learned that many of her friends, fell for that assumption, and ended up hurt, and distraught, over a relationship that never existed. It only took place, in their own minds.

Many a time, she exposed that kind of fantasy to her friends, only to be met with anger, resistance and disbelief. She struggled and listened to her friends' admonishments, that she was a pessimist, a fraud, dark and many other descriptions; for, hidden truth, was best kept there, under the guise of fantasy.

She passed through many relationships with men, who had loved and hated her, at the same time. Loved her, attentive giving, and hated, her independence, of them.

In her later years, as she got older and maybe wiser, she started all relationships, with the same edict, 'We will remain lovers until it is over. I do not want a relationship. I do not hold you, to years of servitude, and you do not have to be my lover or friend, when it is over.'

Men loved that, at first! Everyone of her lovers would go headlong into that relationship. A relationship, that demanded nothing of them, nothing at all. When one of her lovers once suggested that he, "could not stay that long, that evening", he, "had stuff to do, just could not stay"; she ended up, sending him home. He was not allowed to see her, ever again. She did not need the whining, or the complaints.

There were also the men who got upset that the relationship had not evolved.

"What is wrong with me?" was, the mantra.

"Nothing wrong with you," she, would reassure. "That is not, what we agreed on, when we first met."

"But, we get along. Things are good. We like each other…"

And every-time, she tried to explain that she was not interested in anything more than what they started, there would be recriminations and hostility.

In her experiences, no, men did not like being treated, like a piece of meat. That was their God given right, not for women.

So, as things evolved and she evolved, she got more comfortable with her role, her needs and her wants.

Most men, came and went, and her life went on. The one decided to be in it, with her, or deal with his life, without her. Baggage was not, usually a problem, since, it could be worked on.

Not having a relationship, did not mean that she did not care for the person. It only meant, that she did not have to wake up with them everyday; did not have to deal with their bad breath, everyday, their ups and downs, everyday. It meant that she enjoyed the friendship, the sex, the companionship; someone to go to the movies with, someone to cuddle with, someone to talk to, but not everyday.

Until Merrick!

She realized that she wanted to be with Merrick everyday. She wanted to see his face, first thing, every morning; and be the last thing, she saw, as she drifted off, to sleep, at night.

Sharing her table with him, her cup of tea, before a fire, the view from the headlands, as the sun came up, over the East Bay.

She enjoyed having him, invade, her privacy, and her space. There was no space, that she could not, share with him. No space, that was private enough, for him, not to be, included.

Merrick found that unnerving, making him anxious, initially. He found it suspicious, and his self protective instincts kicked in, within the first few weeks, of their relationship.

It took eight weeks from the day they met, for Merrick to give in to his need, his desire, for a solid, relationship.

He accepted her apartment key; and with a handful of his clothes, he stepped through the door.

He moved in.

The End

> *The agony of lovers*
> *burns with the fire of passion.*
> *Lovers leave traces of where they've been.*
> *The wailing of broken hearts*
> *is the doorway to God.*
>
> *- Rumi*

About Sonia Rumzi

Sonia Rumzi was an English Literature major in college; turning to, Medical Heart Technology, for practical purposes. Born in Egypt, then immigrated to the United States; having tipped the scales, since, she has now lived in her, chosen, home country, longer, than her original birth place.

Her interests range, from cooking, to knitting, to oil painting, to photography. She loves to travel, documenting these trips in words and pictures. Adores going to the movies and the theater.

For music, her choice will always be, Baroque, particularly Bach. She practices Prayer, Yoga and Tae Bo daily.

A Mother and a Grandmother, she loves, her daughters and grandchildren.

When she isn't travelling about, with her husband, she lives in California, with him, Steve, the love of her life.

Don't miss the next novel by Sonia Rumzi
(Summer 2011)

Meet Salma (from Simple Conversation) again, in her earlier years. You met her as lover and traveler; meet her as mother and wife. Before Merrick.